THE OLD
NEIGHBORHOOD

ALSO BY AVERY CORMAN

Oh, God!

The Bust-Out King

Kramer vs. Kramer

50

Prized Possessions

The Big Hype

A Perfect Divorce

The Boyfriend from Hell

My Old Neighborhood Remembered

THE OLD NEIGHBORHOOD

AVERY CORMAN

BARRICADE BOOKS
FORT LEE, NEW JERSEY

Published by Barricade Books Inc.
2037 Lemoine Ave.
Fort Lee, NJ 07024

www.barricadebooks.com

Library of Congress Cataloging-in-Publication Data

Corman, Avery.
The old neighborhood / Avery Corman.
    pages cm
    ISBN 978-1-56980-530-5
1. New York (N.Y.)--Fiction. I. Title.
PS3553.O649O4 2014
813'.54--dc23
                                                    2014014005

For Matthew and Nicholas Corman
and for Anne and Moses Cohn

TO BE TEN years old in 1944 was to know one's place in the war effort, to collect scrap paper for the scrap paper drive, save Minuteman war stamps, and memorize the silhouettes of enemy aircraft, then crouch on the roof of a building at twilight hoping to spot a Stuka before it could strafe the neighborhood.

We lived in the Kingsbridge Road-Grand Concourse section of the Bronx in a red brick building on Morris Avenue. Flamingos caroused on the wallpaper in the lobby and art deco nymphs were painted on the elevator door of "Beatrice Arms," named for the landlord's wife, Beatrice. The building's most distinguished citizen was The Dentist, who had an office on the ground floor, the smell of ether lingered in the lobby.

My best friends were Arthur Pollack and Jerry Rosen. We were in class 5-1 at P.S. 86, our teacher, Miss Brenner, was a humorless woman in her forties, her hair pulled into a tight bun in the back. The war had helped her organize an educational philosophy, she went from elementary school teacher to pre-induction officer.

"Stand up, Steven R. Hup-hup! At attention!"

We were children of the homefront. I had just downed my sixth German Focke-Wulf of the morning in my composition book. I rose at attention to the snickering of my classmates, some of whom had been sinking U-boats.

"I said, 'Hands folded on desks,' did I not?"

"Yes, Miss Brenner."

"That does not mean 'Hands writing in notebooks,' does it?"

"No, Miss Brenner."

"I am going to tell you of an incident that cannot be repeated sufficient times."

The Foxhole Story. Again! Arthur Pollack produced a comic groan and Jerry Rosen began to giggle.

"Stand up, Arthur P. And you, too, Jerry R. At attention!"

The giggling in the class was now widespread.

"Stand up, class 5-1. All of you, at attention!"

Miss Brenner had the entire class on its feet as she told her favorite war story.

"The infantry squad was in foxholes near the enemy lines. A rifle shot was heard. The officer yelled, 'Heads down!' Some were slow to respond. Others did not respond at all. Everyone was killed. Except for one man. That man *did* respond. That man put his head down quickly. That man was Corporal Howard Reese, a former pupil of mine, who learned in *my* classroom how to follow instructions. And he lived. And the others died. He wrote to tell me this. And that is an important story. You are to listen to your teacher."

Then she said, in case anyone had missed the point:

"Or maybe one day you will be in battle and not know how to listen."

Suddenly, this time in the telling, she noticed a problem with the story line. She rushed to add:

"That means girls, too. You could be combat nurses."

Arthur, Jerry and I were kept after school for being weisenheimers. We had to write on the blackboard thirty times, "I will not be rude and inattentive," a heavy punishment which kept us out of the first stickball game of the afternoon.

Jerry lived in my building, his father was Rosen's Dry Cleaning on Kingsbridge Road. Arthur was the rich one among us, his father worked in Manhattan for a printing company, and Arthur owned electric baseball. We were Yankee fans, my favorite player was George "Snuffy" Stirnweiss, who led the American League in batting in 1945 with a wartime average of .309. His picture was pasted to the wall above my bed, along with my collection of Dixie Cup covers with scenes of "Our Branches of Service in Action." I listened to Yankee games on the radio, the road games re-created in the studio to the sound of the Western Union ticker: "Grimes hits a high fly" . . . tick . . . tick . . . tick. . . . "It's down the left field line" . . . tick . . . tick. . . . "It's" . . . tick . . . tick . . . tick . . . tick. . . . "A foul ball." Time was suspended in these reports, which came in from such exotic places as Cleveland and Chicago.

My parents, Sylvia and Bernard Robbins, had moved to this neighborhood from the Lower East Side the year I was born. They came north by subway to a new social position in their lives, to an area with parks and elevator

buildings. My father had been hired as an assistant manager of a men's haberdashery store on Fordham Road.
Six feet one with reddish hair, he was slightly stoop-
shouldered, as if he were embarrassed to be taller than
his neighbors. My mother was small and fair with fragile
features, a woman who attempted to manage her responsibilities as she perceived them—to run the household
and be informed. Our family and The Dentist and his
wife were the only people in the building to read *The
New York Times,* not held in high regard in the neighborhood, as it did not have horseracing tips or the comics.

My father, 4-F because of a heart murmur, was an air-
raid warden, out on the streets during blackouts. In his
work, after ten years in the Bronx, he was still an assistant manager in the haberdashery, which meant that he
was but a salesman entrusted to use the cash register.
He was extremely low-keyed in business. The store manager told my mother, "He's too nice."

Angry with my father, my mother confronted him at
the dinner table.

"What salesman should be called nice? They should be
saying you're aggressive!"

"Some of these salesmen—they'll sell you anything,"
he answered, defending himself, turning to me. "Even
clothes that don't fit. I can't do that."

He did not advance in his work or earn the money that
others did, but he was honest, the word in the neighborhood was that people respected him. So he was retained
in his job by a succession of store managers he never
replaced.

Our apartment was decorated modestly, bare wood

floors, mahogany pieces, wing chairs and a greenish tweed couch in the living room. The prized piece was our pushbutton console radio, an Emerson, purchased on time. Some families in the neighborhood went to the Catskills or to Rockaway for the summer, as my mother was given to remind my father. On Sundays we went to Orchard Beach by bus. They argued often over money. I pretended not to listen. My mother never took a job to help the family income because in the neighborhood wives did not work, unless the husband was in the army or dead. Neither the husband nor the wife would have approved of the woman working. This was cultural, a given, in the same way that troubled couples, as my parents were, never got divorced. As I think back, thirty-five years later, remembering that besieged couple and the tired man who was my father, it is astonishing to me that I am an older man now than my father was then.

A major day arrived in my life. Not only did I have permission to go with Arthur to the RKO Fordham for the children's show, five cartoons, a Pete Smith, a chapter, plus the double feature, not only did I have spending money for candy, but afterward we were going to Liberty Bell Bridge and Arthur was planning to let me "go half-ies" on his ringing of the bell. A facsimile of The Liberty Bell was erected on the Grand Concourse in front of the Loew's Paradise Theatre and anyone who bought a war bond could step up on the bridge and ring the bell for freedom. I had not yet been able to save enough for a bond in my war stamp book, but Arthur had rung the bell twice before. A bonus for the bell ringers was to look inside a captured two-man Japanese submarine which was part of the war bond display. When the movies were over we ran to the Paradise, then holding Arthur's bond together, we walked up on the bridge and rang the bell—pals for victory. We peered into the submarine and were intrigued by how small and sneaky the submarine looked. I was momentarily encouraged to change my favorite branch of service from the Army Air Corps to the Navy so I could sink Japanese submarines with depth charges from my destroyer.

In the neighborhood, the sense of participation, of being part of a nation at war, was palpable. People placed white flags with blue stars in their windows to signify a man in uniform, sometimes a double star for two men, or a gold star for a man killed. It was a working-class neighborhood divided between Jews and Irish Catholics. Tommy McPheeley, a stickball friend, said that he liked me even though the Jews killed Christ. I asked how he knew that—since I did not know myself—and he said, "Sister Theresa told us." So the idea was being taught in the parishes in the 1940s, and Sister Theresa said so, and she was a Sister, which seemed to be documentation of some kind. But the religious issue generally was set aside during those years, Jews and Catholics were in the Big Fight together and on the killing of Christ it was acknowledged that, at the very least, the event was pre-war.

On June 6, 1944, D-Day, the schools closed early and we were asked to attend one of the special afternoon services being conducted in local churches and synagogues to pray for the safe return of Allied servicemen. The radio had announced that many would die in the fighting, that it was the biggest battle of the war. I walked with Arthur and Jerry to the Jacob H. Schiff Center near Fordham Road. I was nervous as we entered the synagogue, we were supposed to pray and I had never prayed. The synagogue was crowded with children who had been released from school, women from the neighborhood, and the elderly. The rabbi began the service with a news bulletin, the first beachheads were secure. A children's choir sang hymns in Hebrew and the rabbi recited the Lord's Prayer in English, which was momentarily reassuring, since I had heard it in school. Then came the moment I was dreading. He asked the congregation to pray. I closed my eyes and began to imagine bodies being blown out of the water by enemy mortar fire, blood trickling out of the sides of mouths of soldiers in trenches, bayonets ripping into stomachs, planes streaming into mountainsides, pilots' bodies burning—images reinforced by dozens of war movies, now embellished by my imagination and the ominous quality of this day, that I was released from school on the day of the biggest battle of the war, that many would die in the fighting, that I was to come here to this strange place, ignorant of the rules, and that my prayers—whatever praying was, whatever God was—had been asked for, and the deaths frightened me. I was ten years old and I wanted the war to stop. The romantic adventure of the war ended for me on this day. No longer did I draw pictures of P-38s and German planes in my books. The war had exhausted my capacity for militant fantasy.

On April 12, 1945, Franklin Delano Roosevelt died. In this working-class neighborhood he was revered, the man who had led the nation out of the Depression, the Commander-in-Chief. People drifted into the streets and gathered on street corners to console each other. School was canceled on the day of the funeral, stores closed, strangers passed and nodded, sharing the sense of loss. Our doorbell rang and standing there was our next-door neighbor, Mrs. Cavanaugh, a widow who lived alone. No more than a "Good morning" had ever passed between Mrs. Cavanaugh and the members of my family. Alone in her sorrow, she asked if she might come in for a cup of tea. We sat with the radio playing and listened to the reports of the funeral, none of us speaking. Then Mrs. Cavanaugh began to talk about her life, about the details of her husband's death, she wept for President Roosevelt and for her husband, then excused herself abruptly, never to approach us again or ever again to say any more than a "Good morning."

When Germany surrendered, V-E Day was declared, for victory in Europe, and an avalanche of paper commemorated the event in the neighborhood. People threw paper out of their windows, the fastidious cut it into confetti, children hurled rolls of toilet paper from the roofs. I was with my friends, running through the paper that covered the streets. We kicked it, we scooped it, we tossed it like snow.

The Memorial Day parade along the Grand Concourse after V-E Day was a massive victory celebration. Everyone who could march was there—servicemen on leave wearing their uniforms, civilians from war organizations, the wounded in special cars. Those families whose windows faced the Concourse competed with each other in the sizes of their American flags. Arthur, whose apartment was on the Concourse, invited us to watch from his living-room window. Whenever a color guard passed by, the spectators sitting along the curb would rise and come to attention. Uncertain of protocol and wanting to do the correct thing on this important day, when a color guard passed beneath us, we stood at attention in the living room.

"Unconditional surrender!" the younger children yelled without comprehending the words. Victory over Japan, V-J Day, produced another blizzard of paper in the neighborhood. I was part of the celebration in the street when I happened to notice the gold star mother at her window. We did not know her name, but we had seen her, at times, looking down at us when we played. She opened the window and was holding a small brown paper bag. She emptied it and a little stream of cut-up paper went floating to the street below. She watched as the last pieces fell to the ground, then she closed her window. The war was over.

From December 7, 1941, to August 14, 1945, the people in the neighborhood did their share for the duration. The sons and the husbands, those who were able, went into service, those behind bought the war stamps and war bonds, saved the scrap paper, worked in the ground-observer corps and civilian defense, dealt with rationing and shortages, listened to the radio reports with the same hopes that the war would end quickly so the boys could come home. There was a feeling that the people of the neighborhood had been through something together. I was seven years old when the war began and eleven when it ended. Beyond the imagery, the war movies, the war posters, the war fantasies, what I remember is the sense of community in the neighborhood in those years. It was special and profound and I have never forgotten it.

Chapter **2**

IN THE BRONX in the 1950s young people lined up early to be middle-aged. A tremendous force, greater than the power of all the D trains as they traveled up the Grand Concourse, was generated by Bronx parents to make certain their children went to college to get A Good Job.

"What's to become of you?" my mother said. "Time is running out." I was seventeen at the time. I stood before her with my cherished basketball under my arm, having spent an hour by lamplight in the park practicing one-handed push shots, which I considered a highly profitable hour. I was in my senior year at De Witt Clinton High School, a starting forward on the basketball team and possessor of a varsity jacket, with which I hoped to seduce a girl into going all the way—*actual.* Among the possible actuals were Barbara Semmelman of Taft High School—we had a rubbing-up-against-in-hallways, "inside on top" sexual relationship—and Cynthia Cohen of Roosevelt High School, "outside on bottom"—so near, yet so far.

The owners of the local candy store, Moe and Rhoda Fisher, lived in our building, and when I was small the Fishers allowed me to sit in the back of the store and read comic books without buying, making me something of a celebrity among my peers. Now the Fishers had given me a job part-time in the candy store. "You can't be a soda jerk forever," my mother informed me. I was, by her determination, the only young man under twenty-five in the Bronx who did not know what he was going to do in life. My mother was under pressure. She saw me becoming the financial success for her that my father had failed to be. She assembled a collection of college catalogs that rivaled the number in the school guidance office. I did not share her anxieties about my future. What I considered significant was that I had made my high school basketball team, that I had worked my way up from three-man schoolyard games to the community center league to ownership of a varsity jacket that could be worn on weekends. Now that was personal progress.

"You've never even seen me play. I'm a good ballplayer."

"Everybody knows what they want to be."

"The Shadow knows."

"Morty Papkin knows. He's going to be a veterinarian."

"Morty doesn't realize you have to kiss a sheep before you get your license."

"Stevie—"

"It's true. A soul kiss."

"Be serious. You need a plan."

My role model was not Morty Papkin, it was Adolph Schayes, a boy from the Bronx who went on to be all-pro with the Syracuse Nats and who, in a playoff game against the Knicks, once made 11 for 19 from the field, 12 for 12 from the foul line with 16 rebounds. My ability to remember sports information was of particular interest to Sam the Man, the local bookmaker. Sam Goodstein was a slim man who wore glasses and looked more like an accountant than a person who made book. I enjoyed Sam's company, he came into the candy store to use the pay phones in the back. Sam had seen Hank Luisetti play and sometimes he would watch our schoolyard games— everyone played harder knowing the neighborhood expert was watching. Both Sam and my mother had an interest in my future. Sam saw me in the new generation of bookies and had offered me a route peddling football betting cards. I was not interested, preferring to earn my pocket money through the purity of my egg creams.

"You're breaking my heart, Stevie. With your head, you'd make a great bookie."

"There's no percentage in it, Sam. Bookies don't get draft deferments."

We had a television set in the living room now. The set was on every night. It seemed entire evenings passed with my parents never exchanging a word.

My closest friends were still Arthur Pollack and Jerry Bosen. Arthur was short and rotund, our Eddie Lopat, a dazzling pitching-in stickball player with an array of drop balls he achieved by digging his fingers into the ball like a potter. Jerry was between us in height and build, a speedy end in touch football. I was nearly six feet, the tallest, wiry, light-brown hair, light-brown eyes. I suppose I was a reasonably attractive young man, but my best physical feature, as I saw it, was my one-handed push shot. Arthur, Jerry and I went to neighborhood movies together, traveled downtown to Madison Square Garden for basketball and hockey games on our G.O. cards, took long walks together, and did a great deal of leaning—on lampposts, buildings, and cars as we talked about girls, what they were, how to get them, and what made them crazy.

"You know what makes them crazy?" Arthur said. "You lick them with the tip of your tongue just behind the ear."

"You know what makes them crazier? You put your hand right on it," Jerry said, beginning to laugh.

"Virginity—screw it!" I shouted.

We were laughing so hard it came to the attention of Mr. Veezo, the superintendent of the building next door, who liked to send his killer German shepherd, Hans, to retrieve "Spaldeens" from anyone Veezo caught playing off-the-point at the side of his building, Hans seizing the ball with his killer teeth, and Veezo flamboyantly cutting the rubber ball in half with his pocketknife. Laughter at night in front of his building was as unwelcome to Veezo as boys with "Spaldeens" by day, and Veezo and Hans appeared, prompting our anti-virginity group to scatter, Veezo yelling, "Bums! Laugh in front of your own building!"

"Where you applying?" became the key question among the seniors at De Witt Clinton High School. Jerry was applying to the pharmacy college at Fordham University, Arthur was going to Brandeis University for prelaw, and I was a man without a college placement. I knew I would not be going to an out-of-town college, or even a private college. We simply could not afford it.

"You could have had a scholarship," my mother said, "if only you would have worked harder."

"I might have had a scholarship if you were ten inches taller."

"What do you mean?"

"Well, if you were ten inches taller, I might have been ten inches taller and I might have gotten a basketball scholarship."

"Very funny. It's only your future we're talking about."

I was due for my "Career Goals" interview with the school guidance counselor. I did not tell my mother for fear she would slip past the school guards and show up in the guidance counselor's office. In the neighborhood, to be Jewish and not go to college was to commit some unspeakable act for which they would light candles for you, something on the level of going into the navy or getting a tattoo. If you were good in science, you were a potential doctor. If you were good in math, you were a potential engineer. If you were good in history, you were a potential lawyer. If you were good in English and you were a boy, you were in trouble, because you might have considered liberal arts, and in the neighborhood the liberal arts were not for boys—they did not lead to anything. Girls who went to college were expected to be teachers, except for the few who were allowed to major in literature, in exchange for which their parents expected them to use their superior intelligence to marry doctors. So there I was, preoccupied with basketball and virginity, my grades above average, with my highest grades in English.

"Have you thought about business administration?" the guidance counselor said to me.

He was Mr. Beale, a little man in his forties, in a faded blue suit, the collar of his shirt turning up at the ends like an elf's shoes.

"To tell you the truth, Mr. Beale, I don't know what I want to be."

"Well, you have to *be* something."

I was beginning to get the idea. Mr. Beale suggested, since he could not find a pattern to my grades, that I think about the School of Commerce at NYU or the Wharton School at the University of Pennsylvania, which were both beyond my family's budget, or the business college at CCNY. It seemed to me by now that I was going to end up in business one way or the other, that I was not doctor-lawyer-engineer potential, and I might just as well go to a business college if it would help me get A Good Job. In the Bronx of the 1950s a career choice was required behavior for a young man of seventeen. So I decided I would be a businessman and go to a college of business for the right start. I applied and was accepted at the CCNY business school. My mother was overjoyed—Ronnie Hennessey upstairs had joined the navy—it could have happened to *her*. My father was redeemed, his son was going to college. And I was relieved, I had been placed.

The New York Post published its All-City rankings of high school basketball players. After the first-team and second-team listings, in small print was a long list of ballplayers who were given "honorable mention." This was a courtesy list. Each high school in the city was represented by one graduating senior. My name was there for De Witt Clinton. For several days I had status in the neighborhood, little children would go out of their way to say hello to me, and people congratulated my parents— "I hear Stevie got his name in the paper."

Sam the Man said to me in the candy store:

"Congratulations, Stevie. All-City."

"If you read small print."

"No, it's really something. And you know what else it makes you?"

"What?"

"All-Neighborhood."

"All-Neighborhood. I'll take that. Thanks, Sam."

"So where you going to college?"

"City Downtown."

"City? They don't even have a team now. What's that all about?"

"It's about getting a job, Sam."

CCNY, Fordham, Brandeis—the guys were going to be college men. We wanted to celebrate by going to Poe Cozy Nook, a neighborhood bar. Not being eighteen, the legal drinking age, we had never been served in a bar. To accomplish this would be to officially place our high school years behind us. We went to the Adam Hat store on Fordham Road and bought porkpie hats to look older. On the way to the bar we practiced nonchalance and the ordering of drinks with deep voices. Arthur was not

sure he looked eighteen even with the porkpie so he also
bought a pair of sunglasses.

"How old do I look?" he asked, hoping.

"A young eighteen. Don't worry, Stevie is going to
carry us. He looks eighteen and a half, easy," Jerry said.

"Do I look like Bogart?" I asked, doing a tough-guy
pose.

"You look like Bogart's baby brother," Jerry answered,
and we all started to giggle, not a very effective way of
passing. We recovered outside the bar and entered, hats
slung over our eyes.

"A martini please," I said in my deepest voice.

The bartender gave me a withering look.

"And what about you guys?" I said to the boys, deeply.

"Rye and ginger," Jerry said. Arthur merely nodded,
afraid to speak.

The bartender looked us over, but decided to pour the
drinks. We drank them down, then exploded onto the
sidewalk, laughing and congratulating each other. "That
was the worst thing I ever tasted in my life," I said.

We had gone into a bar and we were served! But in the
other important schoolboy rating, Barbara Semmelman
and Cynthia Cohen never "let." They were saving "that"
for marriage.

"Rock Around the Clock" by Bill Haley and the Comets
was not my song. I preferred romantic love ballads and
worked on my impersonations of the singing voices of
Nat King Cole and Mario Lanza for the counselor show at
the children's camp in the Adirondacks where I worked
the summer before I began college. I also wrote parodies

for the camp sing, which was my ticket to nonvirginity. My big hit was set to the tune of Jimmy Durante's "Umbriago" and was called "Impetigo." "Impetigo, if you got it you go, if I got it, I go." At night after the sing, my summer girlfriend, Carol Ershowsky, counselor for the Iroquois girls, on a blanket on the ballfield behind second base, told me how interesting a person I was, and with her sneakers on, her camp sweatshirt pulled up and her camp shorts pulled down, we did it—*actual*. I fumbled for one of the many "just in case" rubbers I kept in my wallet over the years and which usually turned questionable with age, and I accomplished the actual, hurriedly and inexpertly, but it counted. We made several trips to second base that summer, Carol Ershowsky swearing me to secrecy not to tell anyone in the world, and actually I have not until now. I think we have passed the statute of limitations on that sort of thing.

Carol went off to the University of Vermont and wrote to tell me she was engaged to be engaged and I entered college wondering if people could see the change in me over the summer. I continued to work part-time in the candy store for spending money and in children's camps during the summers. In the neighborhood, people my parents knew were moving to places like Rego Park and Kew Gardens in Queens, and some to the suburbs. We remained. My father was still working as a haberdashery salesman on Fordham Road.

My parents were overinvolved in my college career, my mother with persistent questions about schoolwork, fearful that I might flunk out of school like Morty Papkin, who left his mother in shock and mine in possible

shock. My father's involvement took the form of his reading my college textbooks. I would discover him late at
night reading them as though they were his own.

My parents now seldom spoke to one another. A kind
of language passed between them that had to do with the
dumping of garbage and the buying of groceries. They did
not greet each other, they barely talked. "That's ancient
history," one would say to the other if someone tried to
remember a pleasant moment, or more likely, tried to
blame the other for an injustice. In this way, they created ancient history out of the daily events of their lives.

Half of my college courses were in business subjects and
half in English, history and the social sciences, the idea
behind the curriculum of business colleges in the 1950s
was, I think, to turn out people who could understand a
business story in *Time* magazine. The curriculum was
not demanding and I worked in the business department
of the school newspaper after classes. I ravaged the city's
landscape for cheap dates, ice skating, square dancing,
and I went on "intellectual" dates to Broadway plays, the
last row of the theater, and to the Ascot Theater in the
Bronx, which showed foreign films. I considered myself
a complex person, one part businessminded, one part
intellectual. I was going to be a well-rounded corporation
executive. I am embarrassed to think of myself in those
years, traveling by subway to school each day, wearing a
jacket, shirt and tie because it was what the young businessman would wear. I could not wait to be forty.

Chapter 3

SAM THE BOOKMAKER affectionately called me "Joe College." In my view, "Joe College" referred to people at out-of-town schools who wore white bucks, drove MGs and had girlfriends with straight hair. I was the little kid Sam knew who had read comic books in the back and was now in college, and that was an achievement to him.

"How you doing today, Joe College?"

"Well, Sam, some syrup, some milk, some seltzer and you've got yourself an egg cream."

"That's for now. You're gonna be a big-shot executive."

"Can I bet on it?"

"I'm telling you—the world is losing a fine bookie."

"They still have you, Sam."

"Me? I'm nickels and dimes. You'll do terrific. You've always been a nice kid."

"As Leo the Lip said, 'Nice guys finish last.'"

"Not you, Stevie. You're a class individual."

I did not believe him, not when I went, out of curiosity, to stand under the clock at the Biltmore Hotel at Christmastime where, according to rumor, college people picked each other up, and discovered by eavesdropping that many of them were *staying* at the Biltmore—people my age staying at a hotel. I had budgeted myself to buy an out-of-town college girl a drink.

I became the business manager of my college newspaper, selling and writing ads for local merchants, and qualifying to attend a convention of college editors and business managers which was being held in Detroit. I went by plane, my first plane trip and my first stay in a hotel—for serious panel discussions on "The College Newspaper in America," and even more serious party-going, necking in hallways and, for some, alleged actuals in bathtubs. This was my first exposure to people my age from different backgrounds. I noticed—I did not think I was imagining it—that the boys from the "better" schools were clearly more poised than I, they were better dressed, in tweed jackets and rep ties, while my best jacket was tan linen bought wholesale. I made a move for a pretty girl from Bennington, we were discussing theater and I thought my background did not matter, when someone from Yale broke into the conversation and eventually spirited her away. All those poised people from rich schools. I wanted to rip off my nameplate with the "CCNY" on it. I had never felt so low-class and poor.

Fanny Pleshette helped my confidence. A junior at Barnard, her phone number came to me through a cousin of Jerry Rosen's and I called her in the "You don't know me, but . . ." tradition. Fanny was a chubby brunette who referred to her former boyfriends as "lovers," who lived with her mother in a doorman building in the East Sixties in Manhattan and who had been to Europe. She was on a first-name basis with her parents, Jim and Flo, as in "Jim and I had lunch today . . ." and her parents were divorced. This was not a girl from the Bronx.

She went with me on my under-$5 dates, a category in which I was a true expert—try Czechoslovakian folk dancing. She told me I was intelligent and took me to her apartment when Flo was off on her own affairs. This was the actual actual, in a bed with an adjoining bathroom that had perfumed soap. What passed for a hot time in the old days, rubbing up against girls in hallways, heavy petting in the living room, worrying if the parents would wake up, all that was the activity of a much younger man.

Fanny and I did not survive the school year. During Easter vacation she went with her mother to Palm Beach, Florida, and returned in the midst of an affair with a senior from Dartmouth.

"Why Dartmouth?" I said, wounded.

"It was just one of those things that happened between two people," she said. "I'm sorry, Steve, I like you a lot."

"Well, I think I loved you," I told her before hanging up, which was a highly romantic remark, as well as highly conditional, implying that I was not certain, and in any case, it was past tense.

"One can't always be successful in these matters," I said to Jerry on one of our walks through the neighborhood.

"This is a valuable learning experience." What I really wanted was to learn nothing from it and just be with her.

My senior year was ending and my business career was due to begin. My mother began to leave copies of *Fortune* and *The Wall Street Journal* on my bed with key passages underlined so I could gain an edge on the future. I had decided that advertising was the most interesting of the fields of business I had been exposed to, I did not know of anyone in the neighborhood who worked in advertising, the field was not within the social context of the neighborhood. This was very appealing to me, to be the first, a truly sophisticated person. I made a selection of advertisements I had written for the college paper, took advertisements out of magazines and wrote what could be the next installments in those campaigns, creating a portfolio for myself. "I'm going into advertising," I said to Carla Friedman's mother. Carla was the girl I was seeing, a junior from Hunter College who did not "let" when I dated her briefly in high school and did not "let" now. She was very smart, though, and we went on cultural dates together, such as anthropology lectures at the Museum of Natural History and dance recitals by Pearl Primus.

"Advuhtising, that's nice," Carla's mother said. "Ya hear that, Sol? Davie here is going into advuhtising."

"Stevie, not Davie."

Sol looked up from his coverage of the Dodger game, which he was watching in his sleeveless undershirt.

"Zoomar lens," he said. "Brings ya right in there."

These people, my background—I would be getting as

far away as possible from all that by being in advertising. At twenty-one I had decided the most dazzling job in the world was to be an advertising copywriter downtown and write the travel advertisements that appeared in *Esquire* magazine, cultivated people sipping cocktails in elegant settings. I would look advertising and talk advertising and be advertising and the rich boys from colleges like Yale and Dartmouth would have nothing on me. I would pass in their world. I would get out of the neighborhood.

After preparing my portfolio and resume I took a serious step toward integrating myself into corporate life. I bought a gray hat in a Madison Avenue store. "The Advertising Man," the hat was called. I wore it downtown as I made the rounds of employment agencies. In my hat, at twenty-one years of age, I must have looked like a tall Toulouse-Lautrec.

Arthur, Jerry and I tried to see each other, but with Arthur at college in Boston we were restricted to school vacations. We established a ritual of getting together whenever Arthur came into town for Chinese food at the Lu Wong Chinese restaurant on Fordham Road. This was one of the tonier Chinese restaurants in the Bronx in that it had a bar, six squeaking stools facing a discolored picture of Miss Rheingold. A specialty of the house was chicken chow mein which was served in a gelatinous state.

Arthur was in for a weekend, looking very solemn. At the restaurant he dropped a bomb, heavier than the Lu Wong wontons.

"Fellas, I'm getting married."

He produced a color snapshot of a small, round girl who looked something like Arthur. She was standing in front of a house that appeared to be Tara.

"Her name is Sandy. She lives in White Plains."

"Very, very attractive," I said, as though I were looking at a picture of someone's baby.

"Are you getting married or are you getting engaged?" Jerry asked.

"June. Married."

The information was absorbed in silence.

"Congratulations, buddy," I finally said, and having located the appropriate behavior we shook hands with Arthur.

"She's terrific. And her father is loaded. He's got the largest food-delicacy importing business in the East."

I did not know how a food-delicacy importing business worked, what I understood was that our Arthur was marrying a rich girl from White Plains.

The wedding at the Delmonico Hotel in Manhattan that Mr. and Mrs. Morris Mandell arranged for their daughter, Sandra Linda Mandell, and Arthur Robert Pollack, cost $12,500, the bride's aunt announced while standing at the buffet, which Morris Mandell personally provided from his food-delicacy importing business. Like co-captains, both Jerry and I functioned as the best man. The photographer took a picture of the three musketeers in our formal wear. I thought we looked like a trio of magicians waiting to go on "The Ed Sullivan Show." When the ceremony was over, Arthur told us he was not entering law school after all. His father-in-law was bringing him into the firm for a slice of the Nova Scotia.

I sent letters to thirty-six New York advertising agencies and followed up with phone calls to the personnel managers. I was awarded two interviews. In one I was given an aptitude test and told I was strong in clerical skills and they did not have a job for me. The other was conducted on a couch facing the elevators in the reception area. I was given employment forms to fill out and was told they did not have a job for me. I was registered with all the employment agencies that specialized in advertising jobs, and they did not produce an interview. I may have wanted to get away from my background, but I could not escape my background. An employment agent named Walter Evans, a well-dressed man in his forties with a cynical edge to his voice, capsulized my situation.

"You're starting out with two strikes against you, Robbins. You're from City College. People in advertising want to relate to their own kind."

"I speak English good," I said, hoping he would smile. He did not.

"Maybe two agencies in New York would hire you, Grey and Doyle Dane. And they don't have anything."

"I worked on my school paper. It was like a real job."

"I know."

"I'm very bright," I said, desperately.

"I'm sure you are."

He turned the pages of my portfolio without comment. Then he went through some cards in a file on his desk.

"There's a spot with a bathroom-scale manufacturer in Long Island City. They're looking for a management trainee."

"I heard that with some agencies you can start in the mail room."

"Robbins, tell me something—do you play golf?"

"No."

"Do you play tennis?"

"No. Basketball."

"Basketball. It figures. They don't want somebody from the schoolyard. They want somebody from the club."

On the day of my graduation from college, my mother wept at the sight of me in my cap and gown. My father shook my hand and said, "I envy you your possibilities."

He had to return to work that afternoon, and in a celebration lunch that as much as anything revealed our family as to social caste, we went to a delicatessen with tables, located near Fordham Road.

I rewrote letters to advertising agencies that had already rejected me, I kept calling Evans, the one employment agent who had bothered to interview me. Finally he arranged to send me to the McCann-Erickson agency. I was nervous about the interview for days, but it turned out to be a perfunctory meeting with a woman in the personnel department who said there were no openings, they would keep my resume on file, and did I realize that it was strongly against me that I had not been in the army yet? I was not close to getting a job. I was ashamed of the place where I lived. Was there anybody at the McCann-Erickson agency, or any Madison Avenue agency, who lived in a neighborhood like mine? I hated the fact that I had to put a Bronx address on my resume. I was convinced my address alone disqualified me.

By summer's end, thoroughly frustrated, I joined the army. I found an Army Reserve unit where I could complete my military obligation with six months of active duty. This was not what I had in mind. I wanted to be an advertising man. I had the vision. I had the hat.

I was not exactly General George Patton in the army. A young man who always had trouble with buttons, hooks and buckles, and who is not mechanically inclined, will not find the army a hospitable place. I had one moment of particular notoriety during basic training when our instructor in the lofty subject of "The Assembly and Disassembly of the M-1 Rifle" stopped the class of two hundred to announce:

"We have heah a man named Robbins. Remember the name, gentlemen. Robbins has just done what ah have nevah seen in mah life. He has attempted to put the trigger housing group of the M-1 rifle in—upside down. Now that's a first."

My parents came to visit, "What have they done to you?" my mother asked, noting my short haircut, green uniform, green complexion and barracks cough.

"I'm being integrated into America," I said.

She brought me a salami and back copies of *Fortune*. I closed out my career on active duty in delicious anonymity in my job of distributing clothing to new recruits. The supply hero returned to the Bronx and to the ranks of the unemployed.

Before I was finished with the army, and vice versa, I went into a subway photo booth and had pictures made of myself in uniform. I took the pictures, clipped them to the top of my resume and sent off copies to the people who had driven me into the arms of Uncle Sam in the first place. I wrote across the top, "Back again! Not draftable!" hoping someone, anyone, would think I was, at the very least, resourceful. Walter Evans called me three days later.

"Still around, I see."

"Yes."

"You look terrible in uniform."

"I know."

"Well, you're trying. It was a nice idea for a mailing piece."

He set up an interview with a man named Colby who owned an advertising agency in Los Angeles. Colby had come to New York looking for several people to work for his agency in California. One of the jobs was for a junior copywriter at $75 a week. I went to Colby's suite at the Plaza Hotel. He was a large ruddy-faced man in his late forties, who had in his possession my resume with the army photo attached.

"I like this. It's a zippy notion. Are you zippy?"

"Very zippy. The zippiest."

"A good, zippy answer," he said.

He looked over my portfolio, then examined my resume again.

"I'm looking for New York types. That's why I'm here. Is that you?"

"Is the Pope Catholic?"

"Good. You're showing me a lot of zip."

He looked at my ads again.

"The people I have working for me—they're too slow. You're not slow, are you?"

I had run out of zippy. All I could think of was to shake my head no, zippily.

"That's not an answer," he said.

I was convinced by now that he was crazy and I had no chance for a job here.

"What do you do for hobbies—do you like to sail?"

I was going to tell him the truth.

"I'll tell you where I am with water sports, Mr. Colby. At Camp Indianhead, I cracked the spine of a bark canoe by getting out of it the wrong way."

"Well done," he said." My people all sail—and they're no good."

He told me he would let me know within twenty-four hours. I barely slept. He was eccentric but he was offering a real job, writing copy, not just working in a mail room, and in California, a place no one I knew had ever been.

"You can't take it," my mother said. "It's three thousand miles away."

"We'll never see you, Stevie," my father added.

"It's a real opportunity. And after I get some experience I can always come back."

"You've just *been* away," my mother argued.

"Mother, I can't even get arrested here."

"Don't talk like that. Next thing—you'll get arrested."

My mother was a true fantasist.

Colby called and offered me the position, all expenses paid to Los Angeles. "You're a street kid. I like that. Give me the zip and I'll give you the cash." He may have been strange, but he hired me. I had a job. I was getting out of the neighborhood. I had wanted so desperately to find a job in advertising and could not—because of my background. Now I was being hired because of my background.

My mother nearly went into a coma over the news. "California! Who do we know in California?" My father said, "Congratulations," in a quiet voice. I flirted with the notion of asking Carla Friedman to marry me but I did not believe I loved her, and the idea of going to the frontier, traveling light, appealed to me. I told her the news and she cried. I thought I could have had her for the first time if I wanted to, but I did not take advantage. I left her crying. I felt like William Holden.

Arthur came in from White Plains where he was living and we all had one last Chinese meal at Lu Wong. Jerry, Arthur and I took a long walk through the neighborhood. We were out until two in the morning, not wanting the night to end. We reminisced—the wonderful way the seasons would change, the marbles season, the touch football season, the stickball season, we talked about good times, growing up, girls. Then we stopped in front of the house on Morris Avenue. "I'm going to miss you," I said to them, and we shook hands all around, and trying to be mature, we fought off our tears, knowing we were going in different directions and would probably never see each other again.

Chapter 4

PALM TREES AND no subways. I could not believe I was in a place that had palm trees while the people in my office could not believe I did not know how to drive a car. "It never came up," I said to my immediate supervisor. "If you can get a place close to the office, I suppose you could bike to work," he told me. I did not know how to ride a bicycle either. I took an accelerated driving course, passed the test, bought a used Ford and managed to aim the car from my garden apartment to the office.

The Colby Agency handled the advertising for retail stores, car dealerships, real estate developers and a few California-based household products. By New York standards we were understaffed by about twenty people and, as a result, all of us worked on everything. Within a year, when I might have still been in a mail room on Madison Avenue, I had written radio campaigns that had been on the air locally, advertisements in *Sunset* magazine and commercials for local television. I was very impressed

with myself. I could ride to work and hear my commercials on the radio, "Don't just wave at that housefly. It
doesn't want to know you. Slay it with Marvelspray." I
had a date with a beautician and I sweet-talked the poor
girl not into going to bed with me, but in staying up until
2:17 A.M., with her eyes closing, so we could watch my
commercial of a ballplayer batting a plastic dinner plate
past the pitcher without breaking it. "I thought of that,"
I said, glowing. "Uh-huh," she managed.

Tom Ross was my supervisor. Imported by Colby from
New York, he was a careful copywriter and he taught me
to edit my work. His wife had arranged for me to meet the
beautician whom I managed to bore into not seeing me
again. Once every four months or so Colby would stop at
my desk and say, "How are you doing, Robbins?" I would
say, "Zipping it out there," and he would say, "Good. Tell
Accounting to give you a twenty-dollar raise."

Two new junior copywriters were hired, and Marvin
Liebowitz and I moved up to become senior copywriters.
Liebowitz was from NYU and came into the agency from
New York the same time I did. He was a hyperactive
man, which appealed to Colby. Five feet five, Liebowitz
was a person trying to create an art form out of superla-
tives. His favorite copy lines included: "Incredible beyond
belief. . ." "More fantastic than fantastic . . ." "The biggest sale in the history of the planet. . ." He also had an
exaggerated sense of his social life: "The greatest piece of
tail in Western Civilization . . ."

By his account, Liebowitz lived a life of pre-laid, laid,
and just laid. My social life consisted largely of sexual
daydreams about the girls I left behind. I was learning

a standard lesson of adult life. Once a person is out of school the office becomes his source of social life. In this case, Colby supplied us with a pool of old gray-haired ladies. "They're more reliable," he told Ross. While Liebowitz, according to Liebowitz, met girls at traffic lights, car washes, movie houses, "We were eyeing each other right through the movie, so I made my play and we went home for the real thing." California girls were not dropping off the trees like oranges for me and Liebowitz was experiencing "the best two consecutive days and nights ever. . . ."

He offered me a handout, he was going to set up a double date, "Top of the line. California quality," as he phrased it. Peggy and Sue or Sue and Peggy, I never knew which was which, were student nurses and they spent the night giggling, as did Liebowitz. After a movie and hamburgers, Peggy or Sue kissed me goodnight and went giggling off. Liebowitz had been necking in the back with his date while I drove the car. On the way home, Liebowitz declared:

"Well, I scored again. Best quiet quickie in the back seat of a car ever. . . ."

"Quiet quickie? That may be alliterative, Liebow, but it's not true."

"You couldn't tell, Steve. You were driving."

"Liebowitz, what you need is a definition of terms, or a discussion of the birds and the bees."

In a service grocery store near my apartment, I met Rodi Collins, a divorcee of twenty-one, a thin, nervous woman who worked in the office of a construction company. "I'm going to be a girl singer," she told me.

"You're already a girl."

"That's the expression—in the music business. Girl singer."

During our first night in bed I did my Nat King Cole impersonation.

"Not bad," she said. "Maybe you should be a boy singer."

She stood me up several times, was late for appointments, was on an avocado diet because she said avocados were good for her vocal cords, and claimed Patti Page had taken a personal interest in her career. Needing company, I ignored the oddities. Ultimately I could not ignore her voice. She finally sang for me, "My Funny Valentine," in a thin, cracked voice. Liebowitz would have said, "One of the two or three worst voices west of the Rockies." I had to concede that she was no more a possible relationship for me than she was a possible girl singer.

I went to bars along the Strip, the women at the bars were prostitutes. I was not a native, not a college student, Los Angeles was a sprawling place that lacked a center for a person of my age to meet "a nice girl." I was on my own and I was lonely. I thought the local campuses might be a social avenue for me. If I could have met an older coed or a graduate student I might have been able to outmaneuver the college boys with my professional standing.

A square dance at UCLA was advertised as being open to the public and I went for the fiddling and the calling of Montana Joe Turntree and his Montana Boys. I noticed two blondes in their late teens or early twenties in a corner and I approached one of them. She was about five feet six, slender, her face was soft, a pretty girl with the palest blue eyes I had ever seen. I wanted to say "Excuse me, I may have just fallen in love with you." Instead I tried "Excuse me, didn't we meet once in Montana?" which I thought was an outstanding opening line, considering the ambience.

"I have never been to Montana," she said gravely.

Her friend went off to dance with someone.

"Are you a student at the college?"

"Yes."

"I'm not doing very well, am I? My name is Steven Robbins. And yours is—?"

"Beverly."

"Beverly. Will you be my partner? Please."

She agreed to dance with me and after a while we went out for a cup of coffee. She was a senior at UCLA, an art history major, Beverly Hillman from Sacramento. She had never been east of Nevada. I regaled her with tales of The New Pioneers, meaning myself, who boldly crossed the Rockies to make A Good Living in the West.

I went out with her four times before she would come to my apartment where we necked heavily until my lips were bruised. I had decorated the place with oak furniture and the obligatory 1950s butterfly chair and bullfight posters. I made dinner for us, a beef stew, the recipe off the tomato-sauce can, and I lit candles. I was working very hard to impress her and kept up a constant banter. Now and again she would smile at something I said which I took as encouragement to keep going. When the evening was over, she kissed me gently, took my face in her hands and said, "Why don't you calm down?"

Beverly was quiet, intelligent, I knew she was not going to sit up for my early-morning screenings of thirty-second television spots. We went to concerts, art openings, film series, lectures. Beverly was more widely read in the classics than I, her aesthetic sense was more developed. She planned to take a graduate degree in art history and eventually work for an art museum. I was thrilled to be with her, just to be seen with her. She had such a pure, beautiful face. And she was kind. She brought me books she thought I would like, and she gave me a lovely graphic by a California artist. I had never received spontaneous gifts from a girl before. In the Bronx all my relationships had a feeling of negotiation. Was the girl going to get you to take her to eat *and* the movies, or just the movies? How much was she going to "let" for how much would you have to give? After Beverly and I had gone to bed and sex became part of our lives and not subject to negotiation, I was in a situation unique to me, where kindness between people was important.

"Just like that—you're giving this to me?"

"I thought it would look nice on your wall."

"I'm overwhelmed."

"You're just lucky."

"Yes, I am. I'm very lucky."

I think I was able to bring something to her life as well, some vitality. I was not as manic as Liebowitz, but I was more alive than Beverly's previous boyfriend. His name was Jeremy, a tall, blond art instructor at UCLA, whom I met at an art department tea. He was holding forth on his views of art and artists, several coeds doting on him.

THE OLD NEIGHBORHOOD   41

"Jackson Pollock is vastly overrated as far as I'm concerned," he was saying in a tired voice."Whistler is another one. Some say he was underrated. I can't see him at all."

"His mother didn't think so," I said.

"Are you interested in art?" he asked me patronizingly.

"The art *industry* interests me at the moment. People who make a career out of talking about it."

"You don't seem very happy at this party."

"It's lively enough. If you were brought up in Death Valley."

Beverly walked over and took me away from the group. "Steve, relax. I'm with you, not with him."

For six months Beverly and I spent at least two nights together during the week and every available hour on the weekends. On Saturday mornings we were apart, Beverly rode horses, which I regarded as some California thing, then after that we were together until Monday mornings.

One night before we went to sleep, I said to her:

"I love you."

"I love you? That's what you say? A bigtime copywriter and that's all you can come up with?"

"I can't think of anything else to say. I love you, Bevvy."

"Steve, I love you too."

"Do you?"

"Very much."

"Do you think you could see your way clear to marry me?"

"I think I could."

"God! Who would have believed I could find someone beautiful, smart, blond and Jewish?"

"Well, California Jewish."

"Even so—you don't know how much easier you've made it for my mother."

I watched her until she fell asleep, incredulous that this person was in my life. I had never been so happy.

We went to Sacramento so I could meet Beverly's parents, whom she had been reticent to discuss, she said only that they were "in real estate" and "somewhat interesting."

She did not mention that George and Cindy Hillman lived on a ranch outside Sacramento and had horses in the back in a corral, which was a new level in pets for me.

"You got to have *marzel*, boy," George said. "Know what I mean by *marzel*?"

"I believe so."

"Had an old grandmother, and she used to say, 'You need *marzel*.' And she was tough. Tough as horsehide."

George Hillman was in his late forties, five feet ten, lean, suntanned, dressed Western style with a string tie and a horse's head on anything that had a surface, his shirts, belt buckle, boots. Cindy Hillman was a sturdy little blonde in buckskin who looked like a retired rodeo queen. I was marrying into a family that featured Roy Rogers and Dale Evans. George had chosen to color his Western drawl with Jewish words he could not get straight, as though he learned them from Berlitz. He placed "r"s incorrectly in the middle of words, he missed the "ch" sound, making it "k."

"We got *kutzper*. Biggest brokers this part of the country. You got *kutzper,* boy?"

"Sure do. I'm tough as horsehide, Mr. Hillman."

Phones rang constantly in the house, the Hillmans conducted business during meals, in the middle of conversations. The mood in their home was that of an auction. Beverly's older brother, Freddy, attempted to compete but he did not have the *kutzper* of his father. A moonfaced blond in his twenties, he was slightly shorter and heavier than George. As associate in the family real estate business, he did a considerable amount of smiling.

"You have to be a real *shmurck* not to turn over dollars these days," George told me over dinner.

"We're not greedy, though," Cindy said. "We take time out for the good things in life."

"Your horses," he said.

"And your horticulture," she added.

George filled a glass for me.

"L'Tchayem," he said.

After dinner we walked back to look at the horses.

"Beauties, wouldn't you say?"

"I don't know much about horses, Mr. Hillman. Yours look very large and clean."

"Very large and clean?" Beverly whispered to me away from the others.

"What was I to say? Horses! I thought you just rode them. I didn't know your family actually *owned* horses. What else don't I know about you?"

"You don't know how much I love you."

The showdown took place over cognac later that night in the den, a room that was liberally decorated with the remnants of cattle. George Hillman began to discuss New York City, which he had visited once and hated, it was dirty, the people were rude, and I had begun to be referred to as "This New Yorker here."

"Why don't we talk about Beverly and me?"

"Is there something to talk about, boy?"

"We'd like to be married," I said.

"We've been going together for six months," Beverly said. "And we love each other."

"Now, darling, we hardly know this New Yorker here," George responded.

"Mr. Hillman, I am a college graduate, a senior copy-writer at an advertising agency, I earn one hundred fifty dollars a week, and I love your daughter."

"Everybody loves Beverly," Cindy Hillman said. "That's not significant."

"We were thinking about a fall wedding, Mrs. Hillman."

"A fall wedding!" George shouted. "That's too soon. What am I, a horse's *tukus?*"

"George! What Mr. H . means is we have the Jewish holidays in the fall."

"Oh," I said. "Do you have them flown in?"

A wise guy's remark. I was just too much of a wise guy in those days. I was supposed to generate fast talk in my work and get it on paper and I sometimes did not know when to stop. George Hillman was livid.

"The discussion is over! Nobody has my permission to get married!"

I had mismanaged my meeting with Beverly's parents and I was worried, not knowing how much influence they had over her.

"My darlings," she said to them, "we're of age and we're going to get married."

"Why don't you take some time? Get to know each other better," Cindy said.

"We are getting married."

"I'd like to think about this," George said.

"There is nothing to think about."

"You're not even asking us?"

"No. This is an announcement, Father."

If I did not already love her, I would have loved her. They knew something about Beverly that I did not, how resolute she could be—and they capitulated.

"Well, let's not make a whole *magayla* out of it," George responded.

"Thank you," I said, and I shook his hand.

"Here's to you," Freddy said, smiling and raising his glass. *"Marzel tov."*

We were married in 1958, I was twenty-four, Beverly was twenty-one. To help the cause of family unity, I asked Beverly's brother to be my best man. Beverly's college roommate was her maid of honor, I invited several people from the office, including Liebowitz, who told me at the wedding that Cindy Hillman was "the world's best mother-in-law piece of tail in the world" that he had ever seen. I sent invitations to my friends in New York but I knew there was too much time and distance between us now, and they did not attend. My parents seemed dazed throughout their stay in California, as though they were in shock from all the experiences they had to absorb, that I was getting married, that this place was now my home, that their only child no longer needed them in any discernible way. The weather was scorching, they were inappropriately dressed in wool for the trip, adding to their distress. I pleaded with them to let me buy them lighter clothes—I knew they had tried to wear their very best outfits, which happened to be wool, but they refused my offer. My father's posture was more stooped than ever before. My mother looked pale and tired. I suspected that I had disappointed her. I had the Good Job, but I had not become a doctor or a lawyer or even a CPA. My achievements were based upon glibness.

"Do you like this advertising work?"

"Yes. I'm good at it."

"They pay you well, so you must be good at it."

She touched my face, searching for a child she remembered.

"The newspapers here—they're deficient," she said. "I checked."

"They try."

"Can't you get *The New York Times?*"

"You tend to read the newspaper for the city you live in, Mother."

She was not satisfied.

"And everybody rides here. Your legs will atrophy. Your brain, too."

"I think I can get the Sunday *Times.*"

"You promise?"

"Yes, Mother, I promise."

When I consented to George and Cindy's request that the ceremony and reception be held in their home I did not realize this would be the social event of the fall season in Sacramento—a lawn party, tent, society orchestra with violins, beef on an outdoor barbecue and heavy drinking. Beverly's parents invited over three hundred guests, most of them evidently business acquaintances. When Beverly was busy with her cousins, I broke away from the crowd, walked to the back and leaned against the fence which corralled the horses, observing the proceedings, the open sky, the suntanned faces, the leather, the bourbon. I had the distinct sense of being at someone else's wedding. Beverly slipped away from the others and found me there and we leaned against the fence with our arms around each other.

"It's so extravagant," I said.

"Don't worry. My parents will write it off."

"My parents barely talk to each other. We'll always talk to each other, won't we?"

"Always."

"Do you think your parents have had trouble?"

"I don't think it's within their business interest to do so."

One of the horses began to graze near us.

"Unbelievable. I never thought I'd have a horse at my wedding."

"Let's leave."

I turned to look at her, and brushed her hair away from her face, Beverly at twenty-one, in her white dress, carrying flowers.

"Bevvy, you're so pretty I could cry."

I asked the rabbi to read from Ecclesiastes. Little else made sense to me, and Ecclesiastes in a literary rather than a religious sense. My mother had arisen one night, walked into the bathroom, had a stroke and died at fifty-one. The rabbi was connected with the funeral chapel, my parents did not have their own rabbi, and he performed the $25 special, drawing on bits of information my father and I provided, fulfilling his obligation to himself by informing the small group before him that he had not known the deceased personally.

My parents were without living relatives, just a handful of friends were present for the dreary event. Beverly and I, my father and the Fishers from the candy store drove in one limousine to a cemetery in Queens. After a perfunctory ceremony, my mother was lowered into the grave.

"Goodbye, Mother," I said aloud. "I'm sorry."

I had been all right to that point, handling arrangements with the funeral parlor, being businesslike. As I turned away from the grave site, it all fell apart for me. I began to tremble and Beverly took me in her arms. I was weeping, saying over and over, "She never even saw me play ball. . . she never even saw me play ball. . ."

I had left in a closet, and my parents had not discarded, my old possessions: my first basketball—a leather ball taped at the seams with adhesive tape—my varsity jacket, childhood books, my collection of Dixie Cup covers from World War II, a picture of George "Snuffy" Stirnweiss of the New York Yankees. I wanted these things with me and I bought a trunk which I filled with the items and arranged to have it shipped to California.

I gave Beverly a tour of the neighborhood, she found

it "dark and confining," and after my time on the West Coast, I agreed with her. I was concerned about my father, he had been remote throughout the proceedings, but he announced his best therapy would be to return to work. He planned to take a few days off, then go back to the store. He did not seem in need of us, neither I nor Beverly were in the mood for sightseeing in New York, and we booked our return flight to California. The one expression of emotion from my father over my mother's death occurred when we said goodbye at the door of the apartment. My father turned to me and said:

"It wasn't always bad between us. It was good in the beginning."

Beverly became pregnant later that year. This was not planned, but we decided we could afford a baby, I had been receiving steady raises thanks to my progress in the job and to Colby's eccentricity. When Beverly was in her eighth month, my father called to tell me he was going to be married. His new wife was the widow, Rose Davidson—did I remember her, The Dentist's wife? Rose had "means," my father said, and after the wedding they were moving to Florida. Beverly was too uncomfortable with the pregnancy for a long trip and I went alone to New York for my father's wedding, a small ceremony and luncheon held at the St. Moritz Hotel. The new Mrs. Robbins was old Mrs. Davidson from apartment 1-A, a stout lady with blue hair. At the luncheon, they revealed that Rose was establishing a haberdashery for my father in Miami to be called "Bernrose." They felt it sounded better than "Rosebern." Eventually they would become absentee owners and use their time to travel. Rose's older sister was present and made several remarks about my father being "a real catch." He was charming to all, exhibiting a savoir faire I had never observed in him. "The young marrieds," as the rabbi, winking, called them at the ceremony, said they were going to Israel on their honeymoon. I saw them off at the airport, my father and his new wife bound for Tel Aviv, and I returned to Los Angeles.

My mother was dead. My father had remarried and was moving out of New York. Except for a trunk containing old belongings, all my ties with my childhood and with the neighborhood had been severed.

Chapter 5

SARAH WAS BORN, and I became a compulsive expert on child care and nutrition. I sterilized bottles and nipples like a lab technician, I memorized symptoms of childhood illnesses and read Dr. Spock, the same sections repeatedly to make sure I did not forget anything. I would have nailed roseola on the spot. We bought a small three-bedroom house in Santa Monica and I hurried home from work each day to play with the baby, to place my face against her belly and make her laugh.

Beverly's parents would invade us periodically from Sacramento bearing lavish gifts. I resented these gestures, in a competition with my father-in-law for the attentions of his daughter and grandchild. On Sarah's second birthday George announced they were giving the child her own pony. They would keep it for her at the ranch. I was reminded of the Daisy Rifle contests in the comic books I read when I was small, which offered the winner a free pony. The ads missed us as a market, there was not much call on Morris Avenue for Daisy

Rifles or for ponies. Now my own daughter would have
a pony.

Whenever we visited the ranch, George seemed intent
on getting me up on a horse, no doubt playing out some
scenario with the tenderfoot dumped to the ground to
the delight of the hands. Or perhaps it was that my non-
horsemanship exemplified that his daughter had married such a total Easterner.

"You can't know you don't like it, boy, unless you try."

"George, there is death and taxes—and there is me not
getting up on a horse. You can count on it."

"A bit of a *faggalah,* are you?"

Beverly, George and Cindy planned to go riding one
morning and George suggested I go out on a bicycle. I
declined and he knew the reason.

"Don't tell me. He can't ride a bicycle!"

"We were too poor when I was a child. I never owned
one."

"Never met anyone who couldn't ride a bike.
Unbelievable!"

When we returned to Santa Monica I rented a bicycle and became the local entertainment for the local
children, skinning my knees and elbows and caroming
around the streets, learning to ride—goddammit—but
he was still not getting me up on a horse.

My father came to the West Coast with Rose as part
of a trip they were taking to Hawaii. He seemed to have
straightened his posture, he was tan, trim. Rose looked
a little chunkier and her hair a little bluer—but that
might have been my prejudice about Rose's "means"
not being superior to my mother's naive feelings about

intellect and *The New York Times.* Rose's specialty was sitting. She sat in one position for what seemed seventy-two hours.

"If she doesn't get up to clear a dish," Beverly said, "she gets fruit salad in her lap."

"She's retired," I said.

"We go out for dinner every night," Rose told us, confirming the situation. "When my ex died, I said 'No more cooking.'"

"We don't even have an egg in the house," my father said proudly. "We don't even need one."

I decided to change jobs. The agency had been taking on industrial accounts rather than consumer products and the work required less imagination. It was also difficult to move out of the industrial category and I did not want to become trapped, the advertising business was becoming pathologically specialized. A trade joke of the day concerned a copywriter who went out for a job.

"What have you worked on, consumer or industrial?"

"Consumer."

"White goods or package goods?"

"Package goods."

"What kind of package goods?"

"Cereals and soaps."

"Hot cereals or cold cereals?"

Porter and Bell was my new agency, they had a diversified consumer list including California wines, children's toys, a bank, and a radio station, the accounts to which I was assigned. I considered myself a serious advertising man now. I read market research reports, media appraisals, and in a city where businessmen

prided themselves on their casualness of dress, I wore a
continuous assortment of Brooks Brothers suits, ranging
from gray-gray to gray-green. A very serious type.

Our second child was born, Amy, our second blond
baby. I found Amy's birth a curious measurement of
adulthood. I would now have had more experience in
dealing with infants than my own parents.

In a logistical error, George and Cindy were visiting
us at the same time as my father and Rose, who were
returning from another trip, this time they had gone to
Mexico. The Hillmans were in their buckskin, Bernard
and Rose in haute Miami Beach. At dinner, Rose turned
to Cindy, examined the buckskin and said:

"What kind of dress is that?"

"Comfortable. What kind of hair is that?"

"What do you mean, 'What kind of hair'? Bernard,
what does she mean?"

"It's a rinse," my father said informatively.

We had brought in Chinese food for dinner. Rose
peered at one of the serving dishes.

"Is that black thing pork? I don't eat pork."

"Are you *korsher?*" George asked.

"Sometimes."

"The black thing is a mushroom," Beverly announced.

"I wish I was *korsher,* but I haven't got the time,"
George said.

"*Korsher?* You've got a peculiar accent," Rose told him.
"Where are your people from?"

"Sacramento."

"That's Rumania?" she asked.

We had a definite cultural gap there.

"To the *mishburger,*" George said after a few drinks, later in the evening.

"To the what?" Rose asked.

"Mishpocheh," my father said.

"Such an accent."

"Rose is very direct," my father said apologetically.

George then made his announcement, that when Amy was two, she also would have a pony. He was prepared to come up with as many ponies as we were able to produce children.

"A pony? Did he say a pony?" Rose asked.

"If we have any more kids, we'll end up with a riding academy," I said ungraciously, but who needed his ponies?

"To give a pony to a child! I never heard of such a thing."

"Do you ride?" Cindy asked Rose sarcastically. "I mean—horses."

"I go by taxi," Rose replied grandly.

In 1964 I was thirty years old. I was finding less and less the need to be a wise guy, to make a smart remark so people would notice me. Other things were important to me. I had deep emotional commitments to my wife and our children. On a Sunday morning, Sarah was playing in the driveway on a tricycle. A driver, using the driveway to make a U-turn, failed to see her come out from behind the house, knocked her off the tricycle and against the side of the house. When I reached her she was unconscious and in those first few seconds I did not know if she would live or die. I slapped her cheeks and she regained consciousness—as it turned out she had several broken ribs—but when I thought she might be dead, at that moment I realized I would have given myself for her—they could have taken me if in some way it would have saved my little girl. When something like that happens, you can never again be a wise guy.

On vacations we traveled with the children, mostly to the national parks. I can trace those years by the parks visited. One night at a campfire in the Grand Canyon, the ranger asked how many people were from "back East." "Let's see the hands now, anybody from Chicago?" I was a Californian. I even consented to go skiing. I was on the slopes, struggling with my snowplow turns, as my California blondes in ascending sizes whizzed past me. We joined organizations, liberal causes of the 1960s, including a civil rights group for which I wrote ads and fund-raising letters.

"I've got to keep my mind from turning to peanut butter," Beverly said, and we kept busy with cultural events and a film series at UCLA. I was amused to learn that I was really watching "Neo-realism in European Cinema" back in the days of the Ascot Theater when I went hoping to see Anna Magnani's bare breast on the screen.

Beverly maintained her interest in art, collecting inexpensive graphics by new artists. My collecting interest was in old items like vintage movie posters and old advertising signs.

Beverly chauffeured Sarah and Amy, stayed on top of their school events, took care of car repairs and domestic flotsam and jetsam, which she managed with

efficiency. "Neatness counts," she would say, self-dep-
recatingly. She was another overeducated housewife.
"What good is it," she said, "if you know Giotto is not a
children's game?" We had married and started a family
before she could establish a career and now she was virtually unemployable. Squadrons of art history majors
had been graduating from colleges, competing for the
small number of jobs in the field. She decided to take
education courses so she could teach art to children.
On weekends when Beverly was busy studying and
on those nights when she attended evening classes, I
stayed with the girls. Two little angels in long night-
gowns, smelling of their baths, curling into my lap
at bedtime. It is as though that time when they were
young lasted for about three minutes.

By 1969 I was earning $25,000 a year, considered a top
salary for an advertising copywriter in Los Angeles.
Beverly completed her education courses and walked
right into a state budget cutback and a teacher surplus.
She created work for herself and organized an art play
group in our basement for preschool children. She was a
gifted teacher, imaginative, patient, and after about six
months her play group was beginning to show a profit.
We became the subject of a feature in *The Los Angeles
Times*. The woman who wrote the article was a mother of
one of the play group children, but there we were, shown
on bicycles—"Steven Robbins, 35, top adman, Beverly
Robbins, 32, nursery play group teacher, Sarah Robbins,
10, and Amy Robbins, 8." The article was called "The
True Californians."

"The Robbinses eschew yoga, health food fads, the new therapies. They are a conscientious working couple, professionals in every sense. Their vigor and no-nonsense approach to life is truly Californian. Their industriousness contradicts the myth of a society of vain body worshippers. . . ."

I had come to be the embodiment of a California lifestyle.

Within the week I received a phone call from someone at the Sloan and Vespers Advertising Agency in New York. He was coming into town and wanted to talk to me about "a job opportunity," he said. " Something important." This was an agency that had not even granted me an interview when I was first out of college. We met in his hotel room, I brought samples of my work, including a campaign that had won an advertising award and was reprinted in *Advertising Age*. He had a Xerox of that ad on his desk, along with a copy of the article from *The Los Angeles Times*. His name was Wilton Parker, a formidably handsome man in his late forties.

"Very frankly, we need new blood at our agency."

"I see."

"There's a freshness of approach out here that we like. A California style."

"Good advertising is good advertising," I said.

"Yes, but we're all talking the same way back in New York, very frankly."

He looked at my samples, which covered a wide range of ads and commercials.

"Very frankly, it's as fine as I've seen in a long time."

"I appreciate that."

"Robbins, we're looking for a California type, such as yourself. If we were to hire you, we're talking about copy chief and senior writer at thirty-two thousand on a two-year contract."

"That would be a big decision for me."

"We'd pay relocation costs, of course. I don't know how well you know New York, but I live out on Long Island in a lovely area. We could help you find something with good schools, etcetera."

It was the ultimate get-even fantasy, to return in triumph to the place where I had once been rejected. As successful as I had been in Los Angeles, New York was the center of the advertising field.

Apart from the wisdom of uprooting everybody, I had a serious moral question. I had insisted upon, and was given the luxury of working on, the kinds of accounts acceptable to me. We were, after all, very typical 1960s liberals in our home. I would not work on cigarettes because they were harmful, or on Dow Chemical products because of the napalm. I could make these demands in Los Angeles where the agencies were smaller and the agency politics not as intense as in New York. I expressed these concerns to Parker, he thought about this, then he said:

"Robbins, I'm glad you told me. Very frankly, I respect you for it. That's just the kind of directness I came out to California to find."

Beverly and I discussed the job over a several-day period, she did not know if she wanted to leave California—and her play group was becoming established.

"When is it going to be my time?" she said.

"Maybe you could do it there."

Parker asked if he could see us at the house, a suggestion so blatant, Beverly and I were amused. Obviously, he wanted to check out the corporate wife on home ground. We overpowered him, of course, my beautiful wife and children. We were the family straight out of *The Los Angeles Times*.

"We'd like to offer you the job, Steve," he said. "We'd be willing to pay thirty-five thousand."

"Well, we're still thinking about it here."

"I know it's a big decision. But it's an important position we're offering you, very frankly."

When Parker was in the next room, Beverly said to me:

"Oh, take the job, Steve. You want it more than anything."

"I do, Bev. To go back there—"

"Take the job."

A contract was sent to me within days. I loved the irony. I had been hired to come out to California because I was a New York type. Now I was being hired to come to New York because I was a California type.

The news that we were relocating, that for career reasons I was going with Beverly and the grandchildren to New York, was met with unadorned rage at the Hillman Ranch. "What? Say that again?" George told us and we explained it carefully again. "No. I didn't hear that. Tell me again." We tried to round out the argument, that something was in this for Beverly, too. She would have a chance to create a nursery school in a new locale, her business had been only marginally profitable here.

"Are you hearing all this, Cindy?"

"I'm hearing it."

"I don't know what anybody else is hearing, but I'm hearing bullshit."

"Steve will be making thirty-five thousand dollars a year," Beverly said.

"I deal with people who make thirty-five thousand a month," George replied.

"This is what I want," Beverly told them. "These are my wishes," she said, as she expressed what were *my* wishes.

Beverly and Cindy went out of the room to gather together some of the children's possessions, leaving George to glare at me. Finally, he expressed himself.

"You putz."

"George, this is an opportunity for me. You're a man in business. You can understand that."

"You come out here, you take away my daughter, and now when I got grandchildren, you take them away too."

"We'll see you. There are planes. We'll visit each other."

"She should have married Bobby Grenz."

"Who is Bobby Grenz?"

"He's in real estate. In San Diego. He pisses on thirty-five thousand."

"George, it's not only the money. It's a way of proving myself—"

"You *faggalah*! You *tukus*!"

"George, you know you're beginning to act like a *shmurck.*"

A man with that many horses' motifs on his person must consider himself a physical type, and my father-in-law came at me full gallop, grabbing me, throttling me and trying to bang my head against his flagstone wall. I held his arms and managed to contain him, but he was still trying to push me against the wall. Finding myself in the midst of this rage and assuming George Hillman was not going to suddenly faint with embarrassment over his actions, I decided not to discuss the matter of his oedipal-based jealousy, and I tripped him with my leg. The two of us went down, knocking over an end table and bringing the womenfolk into the room in this scene from a Republic Western.

Cindy fondled George while she yelled, "What have you done to him?" George kept muttering, "I'll kill him," which I had understood from the beginning was his intent. Beverly functioned as the peacemaker, sending everyone off to separate rooms and finally extracting weak apologies from us both.

Later on, my children, tears in their eyes, said goodbye to their horses. "See what you're doing to them?" George said, not a man for subtlety. A few weeks later there was a cold but civil parting at the airport. Freddy carried under each arm the farewell gifts from George and Cindy to their grandchildren, two huge pandas, nearly as large as the children themselves, a last, excessive gesture. Those stuffed toys were pathetic in their size and uselessness and I felt sorry for the Hillmans as I had not before. The children refused to part with the pandas at the check-in counter and after a discussion on policy with the airlines people, the pandas were allowed in the passengers' cabin. The flight was underbooked and the pandas had their own seats, where they sat unblinking, symbols of how I had wrenched my children from home and grandparents. So I came flying out of the West with my guilt, my wife and children who were forced to become uprooted for my vanity and career advancement, with my gray-green and gray-gray suits, and the pandas.

We bought a home in Great Neck, Long Island, a colonial house old enough to have character. My children, suburbanites, made the adjustment from suburban life to suburban life. We located stables in the area and the Hillmans shipped the horses east. The reunion was something out of *National Velvet*.

Beverly made plans to establish a nursery play group in the basement of our house and I took my place in the New York advertising scene. I was like a comic book character—Pow! Bam! Splat! Take that! Take that for rejecting me in the first place! Take that because we were poor and I had to go to City College! Take that because the Ivy League boys got the best jobs! It was not enough for me to be accepted in New York. I had to prove that I was an Amazing New Discovery! Better Than 99 Percent of the Advertising Copywriters in the Field!

Chapter 6

THE **ADVERTISING AGENCY** business in New York had changed while I had been away, the old line white Anglo-Saxon Protestant character of the agencies had been eroded, rock music played on radios in the art departments, beards were in evidence, Jews. Our agency even had a Jewish account executive, which in the 1950s would have been like assigning an Orthodox rabbi to the Schick razor account.

In the early 1960s, some of the smaller agencies began hiring Greeks, Italians and Jews for the art and copy departments and these first people through the door made an impact, their work was fresher and more creative than the basic material turned out for so long by the old line types. After a while the larger agencies joined the trend and hired the ethnics. By the time I returned to New York in 1969, kids were the next group that was "in"—young people barely out of college were being employed at large salaries because it was the era when young people were presumed to have The Answer.

He stood before me, the personification of the Youth Revolution, Frank, in his mid-twenties, wearing dungarees and a T-shirt that said "You are what you eat." My job in the agency was to write ads and commercials and supervise the work of other writers in my product group. Frank had been assigned a television commercial for a wristwatch account, and he brought a storyboard into my office.

"This just needs your okay," he said.

The storyboard showed a man on a street corner at night, looking at his watch. The man looked at his watch again, then again, and the commercial ended with the name, "Baldwin Watches," on the screen.

"What is it saying, Frank?"

"I can't explain it. I feel it."

"It doesn't say anything."

"It's a sense, man."

"Well, I sense I have to turn it down."

"Are you kidding me? Nobody turns my stuff down."

"Frank, I like copy that says something. Maybe you could be more specific."

"This is an award-winning commercial, man."

"I'm sorry."

He returned a few minutes later with another idea, a commercial that showed a watch on a dresser, just the watch, with the sweep hand running for the length of the commercial and then the name, "Baldwin Watches."

"This is my best shot," he said. "I'm drained."

"It still doesn't say anything."

"It's symbolic. The watch represents time passing."

"Time passing? How long did you work on it, five minutes?"

"That is a great commercial."

"Maybe it's the change in time zones, but I don't get it."

One day I walked into the men's room to see two copy-writers smoking pot on a coffee break.

"Hi, fella," one of them said to me dreamily.

"How are you?"

"We're going to the movies for lunch. Care to join us?"

"No, thank you."

"Fellini."

"I'll say."

Within a few months I had reached the point in the agency where people at a water cooler scattered when I came down the hall. I was called "Mr. California" behind my back, as cutting a pejorative as New Yorkers could express. Coming in from the outside, it seemed to me that the work being done in New York was excessively clever. I did not like advertising that was so cute it called attention to itself. If I disliked the advertising, it is fair to say that the people creating it came to dislike me. Parker took me out to lunch to tell me about the morale problems in my group.

"The younger people—they feel you don't relate to them."

"They're children of television. Some of them have thirty-second attention spans."

"We've got a mixed bag on our hands, Steve. The cli-ents are reasonably happy with your work, but some of *our* people are not, very frankly."

"Maybe I have different standards."

"Since you're from California, they thought you were

going to be looser. They call you 'Mr. California.' Did you know that?"

"I didn't know." And I started to laugh.

"Why does that amuse you?"

"I graduated from CCNY."

"Really?"

"City, Downtown."

"Oh, my! We never hired anybody from *that* school," he said, in a recidivistic response.

The kinds of campaigns I recommended to our clients and the ads I wrote were very competitive, as competitive as I was. Agencies had always referred to other companies' products as "Brand X" or "Brand Y." I started placing the competitors' products *in* the ads, full labels showing. The advertising trade papers began to write about this and letters appeared, pro and con. Our agency, in pursuit of cleverness, had been employing a cute headline and a few short sentences in the print ads. I began to lengthen the size of the copy, adding more technical information and more details about the products we were advertising. The writers in my group rebelled because they were required to spend more time learning about the clients' products. We had arguments within the agency, and some of the arguments I won and some I lost. Eventually one of our accounts, dissatisfied with my approach, dropped the agency, and at the end of the second year of my contract the agency dropped me. I was "controversial," but more trouble than I was worth, "very frankly."

I had a new job in one week. Young & Rubicam hired me as a creative director at $42,000 a year and set up a product group specifically for my approach: advertising that was directly competitive and that contained specific information about the products.

Consumer rights groups had been focusing on vague and misleading advertising—and here I was, an advocate of the public's right to be informed. I ended up having it both ways, with the reputation as a maverick advertising man *and* a consumer advocate. I had the prestige, the money and the better suits that went with the job; I also had the moral position. My name appeared in the advertising columns, I won awards, Beverly and I went to industry dinners, I made speeches to the trade on "Truth in Advertising," and the story should end right there. I take the salary, the stock options, my wife and I build additions to the house, and as an advertising notable, I write a book on advertising which the students read at CCNY, bringing my career full circle.

But I was a very competitive man. I had to be good, better, best. I could advance only to a limited degree within any advertising agency that hired me. As I moved up the corporate ladder, I would have been obliged to answer to the needs of the corporation, to work on campaigns and products I thought were unacceptable. So in 1972 I joined with Ray Tolchin, a media expert at Young & Rubicam, and we formed our own advertising agency, Robbins and Tolchin. A *New York Times* article called us "The Truth in Advertising Agency." On the basis of our reputations we signed several accounts to our roster. At thirty-eight I had become the president of my own advertising agency and that year my wife joined a consciousness-raising group. They ended up having equal weight in our lives.

"I'll give you Brownie points for taking care of the children. You've always been good about that."

"So I *have* helped."

"Helping is an obsolete word. Sharing is what we're after."

"We are?"

Beverly insisted that although her work with the play group was nearly a full-time job, she still had to run the household, deal with the plumber and the roofer, look after the children, who were now twelve and ten, see to their riding classes and their dance lessons—that the house was basically her account.

She met with her group every Wednesday night: Beverly, three housewives, a single woman who owned a dress shop, and a teacher. I thought that the group might have given me credit for being faithful to my wife. My partner, Ray Tolchin, was making such use of his secretary's time, he found it more convenient to leave his wife for his secretary. I had followed Colby's practice, my secretary was efficient and sixty-one years old. The group decided that I was merely a faithful sexist. Men such as I, who were out of the house much of the time, were to begin undertaking specific duties each week on the order of calling the plumber and doing the shopping for a certain number of meals.

"Bevvy, it's like I'm back in Bunk Chickasaw. You want Monday morning, mop bathrooms, Wednesday, straighten cubbies?"

"I want you to take over two meals a week. I want you to make all babysitting phone calls. I want you to do all the Saturday shopping for the house."

"Bevvy, I gave at the office. The secretaries won't bring the men coffee anymore."

"I'm serious, Steve. The girls will have to do more, too. We're going to get their little consciousnesses raised also." Her arguments were unassailable and eventually I became a more liberated man. Even the group thought so, Beverly reported to me, and I took over many of the chores that automatically had been assigned to Beverly. However, I resented the group deeply, not over the issue of equality in our household—there I conceded Beverly had been right. I resented Sisterhood, the late night phone calls she conducted with other people, the very length of those conversations. I never talked to anyone on a nonbusiness subject for such periods of time. Ray Tolchin was a business friend. We saw enough of each other during the day that we did not care to socialize when the day was over. I was friendly with people who worked for me, but we had sports page conversations. Except for a few neighbors with whom I shared lawn talk and zoning talk and occasionally dinner party talk, I did not have any close friends. This is what I resented most, the intimacy Beverly had with her group members, an experience that excluded me and for which I had no equivalent.

I was like a child peering into a toy store window.

"What's going on in your group these days?"

"Nothing much that I can talk about."

"Well, what's your latest topic?"

"Oh, sex."

"What do you mean, sex?"

"Sex—the having of it, the not having of it."

"In detail?"

"Steve, the idea behind a consciousness-raising group is for us to *share* our feelings and our experiences."

"Bevvy, have you been sitting in that group talking about *us?*"

"We've all been talking about our sex lives."

"What part?"

"Steve, why don't you stop probing?"

"I'd like to know. I don't talk about these things with the people in my office. I'd like to know what you're talking about in your group."

"Well, how often we do it, and what I like that I don't get, and what you like that I don't like, and why we do, and why we don't, and my orgasms, and how long you last."

I must have looked like it was taking about ten minutes for the information to be recorded by my brain.

"I'm going to faint," I said.

"You shouldn't have asked."

"I'm going inside to take a shower now. There's a very strong chance I will never come out."

We survived Beverly's consciousness-raising group. The group lasted for six months, which Beverly said was the normal life span. When it was over, Beverly wanted more for herself than modest household gains. Encouraged by the others, she had chosen to assert herself in her career as she had not done before.

"I want to make my work as important to *me* as your work is to *you.*"

"You should, Bev."

"Are you just saying that, or do you mean it?"

"No, I mean it. So long as we don't go Swedish and *I* have to stay home."

It was all very sophisticated and modern and egalitarian. And now we were to have *two* ambitious careerists in the family.

Chapter 7

BEVERLY'S IDEA WAS brilliant. She conceived an art school for children, a preschool program for tots and an afterschool program for older children. The uniqueness of Beverly's idea was that she did not organize this in a traditional way, making it an arts-and-crafts group with a whimsical name like "Tiny Tots' Glue Fun." She created a program identical in its fundamentals to a college-level art program—art history, theory, painting, sculpture, but adjusted for a child's comprehension. "Children, these cutouts are just like the things you'll be able to do here," I heard her telling a class. "They were made by a very nice man named Mr. Matisse." The atmosphere was kind, loving but never condescending. The children loved her, she was gentle and patient, and the parents respected her. To the upper middle class of Long Island, here was day care without guilt. The children of suburbia were occupied with Culture.

She called her school "The Nassau Institute of Children's Art." We worked together in the beginning, I

helped write copy for mailing pieces and for ads that
appeared in local newspapers. We placed posters on community bulletin boards, on lampposts in shopping malls,
in merchants' store windows. Along with the encouragement I offered, that was the extent of my contribution.
The school became successful because of Beverly's inge-
nuity and personality.

She went out at night to people's homes, talking to
them about her program. She permitted children to
visit the school for trial classes, and they usually chose
to return. She tried to find new ways to expand upon
her premise, to make the school a center for children's
art education. She made contacts with local artists and
invited them to speak at the Institute, and the children
visited the artists' studios. She arranged Saturday bus
trips to New York City and took the children on museum
and gallery tours. She organized one-man shows with
the children as the artists: "April 9-15, Jennifer Bodnick,
Age 10, Watercolors." Beverly expanded into other areas,
devising an art therapy program for exceptional children
and art classes for senior citizens. Then she arranged to
receive state subsidies for these programs.

Beverly had begun with rented space in a store, and
by working long hours, nights, weekends, and by being
resourceful, she had developed the Institute into an
enterprise that now required a two-story building, which
she leased—and she employed a staff of four full-time
teachers, a bookkeeper and a secretary.

In my career, the agency had grown from a "creative
boutique," as people in large agencies were fond of call-

ing upstarts, to a small-to-medium-sized agency in 1977 with a good reputation in the field. I was still primarily involved in the creative side of the agency, but I was obliged to spend much of my day in meetings. Under pressure as the president of the agency, I was drinking more than I should have. I had a system with a waiter at my regular restaurant. He was under instructions to keep my glass filled with white wine spritzers. I never had to ask for a drink, so it would not seem as though I was drinking to excess. I also had the rationale that the wine was diluted with club soda, but after a two-hour lunch, I might have had the equivalent of a bottle of wine for myself. At night, if I worked late, I opened a cabinet bar in my office and moved on to hard liquor. I gained weight, I seldom did any exercise on weekends, occasional yard work, my bicycle had long since rusted. At forty-three I had the beginnings, or a stage beyond that, of middle-aged paunch.

Tolchin kept himself in far better condition than I by swimming at a health club and by having continuous liaisons with young women, who seemed to decrease in age as we got older. He advised me to have an affair.

"Keeps you in shape," he said.

"Why would a man with a wife who looks like Bevvy have an affair?"

"I've got a few answers for that."

"I don't think I want to hear them."

"Well, I guess you're lucky, having Bevvy. But you're also getting fat."

Why would a man with a wife who looks like Bevvy . . . but our sex life was not out of a gothic romance. We

made love usually on Saturday nights, sometimes on a
Friday. In a typical week, Beverly was exhausted and
ready for sleep at ten-thirty, the bed cluttered with last-
minute notes and papers, while I was making a final
check of the work I had brought home. We were very
busy people. My forty-third birthday was celebrated four
days late, first I had to attend a trade convention in Chicago, then Beverly had to participate in an art teachers'
seminar in Washington. We went to a French restaurant
on Long Island. It was like a business meeting. Beverly
brought me up to date on the latest developments in her
work, and I did the same for my work. We spent a few
minutes in token social conversation, talking about the
children, and then, having exhausted the main topics of
conversation, we sat in silence. We found a few minutes
more of discussion on real estate, Beverly's parents had
advised us to build a swimming pool on our property, "A
swimming pool increases your land values, boy." I was
opposed, since it was George's suggestion. I also thought
it would cheapen the appearance of the property. So Beverly and I discussed the pool, then we went home and
made love, it was Saturday night and on the agenda.

We were a picture couple, disregarding my paunch.
Beverly looked even more beautiful than when she was
younger, she had an aura that came with her success.
When we went to industry dinners to see our agency win
its customary creative awards, she looked outstanding.
And when I stood with a forced smile at the community
events Beverly was obliged to attend, people deferred to
me, my name and sometimes my picture appeared in the
business pages of *The New York Times*. And I always

wore good suits, no longer gray-gray from Brooks, imported tailoring from Andre Oliver. We were two local stars, but we were evolving to a relationship that was less a marriage than it was a corporation.

In the middle of a night I awoke with deep feelings of anxiety and I shook Beverly, who was asleep, and I said desperately:

"Bevvy, what's happening to us?"

"I don't know."

"What can we do?"

"I don't know."

We held each other and we fell back asleep again, and in the morning, like a nightmare, the problems of our relationship were ignored, and we went back to the busy life of two professional people, as we tried not to notice that we were drifting away from each other.

For Christmas 1978 I received from my family a gas-fired barbecue grill, a chef s hat and an apron that said, "Get 'em while they're hot." The grill was, in part, a serious gift. I had insisted that one night a week we had a dinner together, as a family, in our home. Long past was our custom of taking family vacations, the children had been going to sleepaway camps and during the year they were involved with their social lives. Beverly and I were preoccupied with our careers. In our house, a conversation between any two people on a subject or a feeling, as opposed to a logistical problem or a monetary request, was a unique event. Monday night was the time chosen for the family, and for that meal, which I prepared, we were all obliged to remain at the table until dessert and remind each other that we all still lived there.

Sarah, seventeen, was a high school senior and was stunning. Tall, graceful, with long blond hair, she read *Vogue* and was more sophisticated than her years. Boys collected at the doorstep like dust. Amy, fifteen, was working against her sister's type and was wholesome rather than chic. She kept her blond hair short, and she was animated, whereas Sarah preferred to be cool. Sarah had been a Vietnam protester, her current cause seemed to be her personal appearance. Amy passed through causes the way Sarah passed through romances.

"Some of us are going over to Shoreham on Saturday," Amy announced.

"Be careful," I said.

"It's just a march."

"Daddy, don't you think you can come up with something better than 'Stop Nuclear Proliferation'?" Sarah asked, indicating a button Amy was wearing.

"But I'm sure Daddy is in favor, right, Daddy? You're a corporation man, you work for corporations and Corporate America wants nuclear power plants," Amy said.

"I'm not necessarily in favor."

"Advertising is the tool of the Corporate Megalopolis," she declared.

"The what? I think you've got your labels a little mixed up there."

We finished the meal with small talk and as everyone was about to scatter, I said to Amy:

"Whatever you think of your corporate father, I can do better than 'Stop Nuclear Proliferation.' It is, after all, what I do."

"Go ahead then."

"Nuclear Energy's a Bomb."

"Not bad," she said. "I mean—pretty good." And I managed to gain a grudging smile from her.

Beverly's local stature earned more dinner invitations than we could accept from people in community organizations and the parents of children who attended the Institute. We were greatly admired as a couple, people wanted us gracing their tables like salt and pepper shakers.

Because of the demands on our time, we established priorities in our domestic life—we became specialists at that—and appeared in public together only after determining that we both needed to go. "I need you for the Lamberts' dinner party," Beverly might say, and I would attend, fielding the inevitable discussions about advertising—people often had a favorite commercial they had seen. I would be moderately charming and get moderately sloshed.

We were constantly busy with our obligations. Beverly was out several nights a week, I worked late at the office, we both traveled. Days could pass before we would catch up with each other with both of us not too exhausted to talk for more than a few minutes. We reached a point where our secretaries spoke to one another to remind us of any social commitments we may have had together. We did not like the idea, our secretaries as surrogates, but we did not resist, since it happened to be efficient.

My first boss, Colby, had once said when he found me working late in the office, "They don't pay you something for nothing." As the president of an advertising agency, and with Beverly the head of a children's art center, we were living at a high level of achievement, but also of pressure and responsibility.

I always kept a pad near my bed in case I thought of a copy idea before I fell asleep. One night I jumped out of bed to write down "We never stop working for you," to be the basis for a commercial for a brokerage firm with our agency. The commercial would show a broker bolting out of bed, jotting down an idea.

Beverly's pressures were similar. She was busy administering the school's activities, working on curriculum, teaching the children, reading books and reports on art education and child psychology, making speaking engagements, dealing with parents. Then she thought of a concept for an enterprise that became nearly as profitable as the Institute itself—a summer camp. She rented unused space behind the Institute, added play equipment, a swimming pool, developed a summer curriculum, hired counselors who were art teachers, and the Nassau Institute of Children's Art Day Camp was established.

Leisure time had to be scheduled on the calendar. We planned a Saturday of antiquing in Connecticut, which was postponed three times before we were able to go. At an antiques shop, Beverly saw a landscape that she liked by an unknown primitive artist. The painting was too primitive for my taste and too expensive at $400.

"I just don't like it," I said.

"I do. I'll buy it for my office." And she paid for it out of her business checkbook.

At another antiques shop I found something I liked that she did not, an old-fashioned soda-parlor jar for straws.

"Where would it go?" she said.

"In the kitchen."

"There's no room."

"I'll put it in *my* office then."

I was having difficult days at the agency, Tolchin and I were arguing bitterly. He was in favor of chasing every account on Madison Avenue that was having second thoughts about its advertising agency, so our company was spending inordinate time on new business presentations. Since a main selling point for our agency was my creative participation, I had begun to feel as if I were a machine, cranking out copy.

Many of the new accounts Tolchin had been pursuing were the type who jumped from agency to agency, taking an agency's best ideas, then dropping the agency for the next. I was opposed to working for these manipulators, and I also was intent on keeping our client list strong in products with competitive advantages. I had weakened against my partner's pressure and we took on a soft drink which was a blatant copy of 7-Up. This was the kind of account I had always objected to, a product that had no competitive advantage and nothing specific to promote.

"You can't be so rigid," Tolchin said. "Business is business—and we can use the business." And I relented.

The people with whom Beverly and I were friendliest, John and Pat Cleary, lived across the street. John Cleary,

a pipe-smoking tweedy man in his forties, taught political science at Stony Brook, and when we were together
at least we could talk about political events. The Clearys
did not have children. Pat Cleary, a petite plain woman,
kept busy as a housewife. Their house was spotless,
laboratory experiments could have been conducted on
the premises. One night Pat caused a moment of awkwardness during an unserious discussion of the forms in
which we would like to come back in our next lives when
she said, "I'd like to come back as Beverly."

We had joined the Clearys for dinner at a restaurant.
I had too much to drink, as was my custom, and the following morning I awoke with a hangover. "They're here,"
Beverly called out while I was showering. I had forgotten
that she had said the previous evening that people were
coming to the house for breakfast. I went downstairs in
my groggy state to see a busload of Japanese tourists on
the back lawn, eating lox and bagels, which topped pink
elephants on parade.

"This is my husband," Beverly said, and I was greeted
by smiling faces and clicking cameras.

They were educators on a tour, they had visited the
Institute and now Beverly was showing them the way
we lived. I withdrew to the kitchen to read a newspaper.
I noticed through the window one of the men, a sensual
type, doing considerable smiling and touching of Beverly's waist. I did not see the educational value in that.

"Hello, cuties," I said, breaking in on them.

"Mr. Namruchi, my husband, Mr. Robbins."

"I greatly appreciate your lox and your bagel, sir," he
said in perfect English. "Also your wife."

He was too suave for my hangover.

"Help yourself to the former," I said, leading him to the buffet.

"Steve, that was rude."

"Well, what were you two discussing?"

"A pool," she said, sarcastically. "He suggested we build a pool."

There had been a time when the smallest victories were a reason for Beverly and me to celebrate—my first pay increases, the first enrollments at Beverly's school. We took our achievements for granted now. Beverly was to speak at a meeting of the Nassau Women for Equal Rights—I decided not to go with her and worked late at the office instead. A few weeks after this, I was going to an advertising industry dinner, our agency would be winning an award again, and Beverly chose not to attend—she was preparing to head a workshop at a teachers' conference.

There was a surprise citation at the Equal Rights meeting, Beverly was named Nassau County "Woman of the Year," and at my dinner I was given a personal award "for promoting the concept of Truth in Advertising." Neither of us was there for the other, we drove home alone with our awards those nights.

Chapter **8**

BEVERLY AND I had always required two "yes" votes on any major decisions—the unwritten contract between us had been that we each had veto power over the other. In the early years of our marriage we had consulted even about such modest items as my shirts, Beverly's shoes—we went shopping together or we brought the items home for the other person to see—"Should I keep it? Is it too expensive?" Now we shopped for ourselves when we could find the time, we bought what we needed and paid our own bills when they came in.

The girls did not have access to our credit cards, as was the case with some families, and I insisted Sarah and Amy now work during the summers to earn spending money. When the school year ended, they would be counselors in a children's camp. Sarah was graduating from high school, and after her camp job, going to college. Beverly suggested that we buy a new typewriter for Sarah, the one she had was barely usable.

"Fine. We can replace it," I said.

"I think we can improve on that," Beverly answered. "If we're getting her a typewriter, it might as well be an electric."

"Why does she need an electric? They're expensive."

"We can afford it, Steve."

"A portable nonelectric typewriter is good enough for a teenage girl."

"But she can have something better."

"You're talking about hundreds of dollars."

"Three hundred dollars."

"Forget it. She doesn't need a three-hundred-dollar typewriter."

"With the money we earn around here, it's nothing. What am I working for if I can't give my daughter something extra every once in a while?"

"I never even *had* a typewriter when I went to college."

"Just because you didn't have it doesn't mean she has to do without it."

The issue was not discussed further and then two weeks later I returned from work, Sarah greeted me at the door warmly, saying:

"Daddy, thank you!" and she brought me to her room where on her desk was a new Smith-Corona electric typewriter.

"Use it well," I managed to say and walked quickly out of the room, looking for Beverly, who was in the bedroom. "Bev! You knew how I felt!"

"I disagreed with you."

"And you just went ahead and did this?"

"What's the difference?" she said. "I bought it with *my* money."

For fifteen years Beverly and I had never spent a night apart, except for the times when Beverly was in the hospital with the births of Sarah and Amy. Our separations had become routine now. I had just returned from a business trip to Dallas, Beverly was in Philadelphia at an art therapists' conference. I made a dinner of scrambled eggs for the girls and me. Sarah went out on a date, Amy left for a planning meeting to save the Atlantic Salmon.

Feeling lonely and in need of company I called John Cleary and asked if I could come by for a drink, a request I had not made before. He was amenable and I went to the Clearys' house. The centerpiece of the house was John Cleary, who was served his meals, never had to lift a plate, and received his evening newspaper and scotch on the rocks in his lounge chair. Pat Cleary served us cheese, crackers and drinks and then withdrew, leaving the men to have man talk.

"You have the perfect life here, John. It's the nineteenth century with color television."

"Except you get Pat with that."

"I wouldn't knock Pat."

"She's vapid."

"John, I came here to say I've got business problems and my marriage is just as bad. Please don't tell me you've got troubles of your own."

"You and Bevvy, problems? I can't believe it."

"You don't know how lucky you are."

"You don't know how I've envied *you*. To be married to someone like Bevvy. Do you know where Pat is right now? Ironing my underwear."

"She irons your underwear?"

"True."

"You must have outstanding underwear."

I intended to talk about my relationship with Beverly, but I did not know how to begin and I felt disloyal discussing her with John Cleary. He was untroubled by loyalty to Pat, he told me that her banality had driven him into an affair with a young woman on the faculty at Stony Brook, then he went on to complain about the young woman. He continued with his complaints, moving on to academic life. At first I thought he was performing a comradely act, telling me about his situation to make me feel less troubled about mine. But he went on drinking and talking about himself, dragging out petty grievances about colleagues and university bureaucracy, and I drank along with him. Where were those wonderful conversations I had in the old days with my buddies, the walks we took when we talked and listened to each other and helped? "Walk me," you said to a friend and he walked with you and you talked. He took the time to go where you were going just so you could be together. Talking to John Cleary, my supposed friend in adulthood, was a game, how many points he could score in his own behalf before he would be required to listen to you. I excused myself, and moving unsteadily from the effect of the scotch, went back to my empty house and fell into a troubled sleep.

I went through a particularly hectic period—client meetings, deadlines on my own copy, overseeing the work of other copywriters, who were also overworked—three of our copywriters had been out for nearly two weeks with the flu. I had a meeting with a young art director and the account

executive for one of our accounts, a manufacturer of frozen
pizzas made by a new fast-freezing process. That particular day an auction of graphics and posters was being held
at Sotheby Parke Bernet. I had seen in the catalog a World
War II poster that I remembered from the 1940s, "Buy
War Bonds," with the flags of the Allied nations. I wanted
the poster, but I could not attend an auction in the middle
of the day, so I phoned in a bid of $200, a few dollars above
the estimate. The auction would just have been ending
and I was eager to call and find out the result, but I had to
be at the meeting. Ideas were exchanged, the account man
pointed out that the client had a limited budget, they were
straining their resources to advertise on television. I was
having trouble concentrating. Finally, I said:

"Look. Why don't we do something different? You have
a black screen, voice over, white type with the words:
We don't have much money for advertising. Next frame:
How do you advertise frozen pizza anyway? Next frame:
You have to eat it to know what it tastes like. Next:
Carmella Frozen Pizza is made by a new fast-freezing
process. Next: It's very, very good. Next: We don't want
to overproduce this. We put our money in the product.
Next: Carmella Pizza. Very, very good."

"That's very, very good," the young art director said to
me with a look of awe.

"Perfect," was the account executive's comment.

All I had wanted was to get out of the room. And I did
not get the poster.

We also did the advertising for a national insurance company. The company offered an insurance program for

senior citizens, and the client, who was socially conscious, had decided to run a public service campaign in praise of older people. I worked on the campaign on and off for several days, to the exclusion of other work. Tolchin said the time I was spending on this was unwarranted, it was low budget, the agency would not be making much money on it and other projects required my attention. I could not let go of the material. The project had a moral quality to it and I wanted the ads to be as good as they could be. "Robbins' Folly," Tolchin began calling it. Finally I came up with a headline that I liked: "Old age—it's not a disease, it's a national heritage." The ad would then discuss the knowledge and expertise of senior citizens, and for the artwork I thought we could use documentary photographs in the style of the old Farm Security Administration images. A photographer could go out and take pictures of senior citizens across the country in realistic settings. This would have been a slow process and could have become expensive. Tolchin, supported by the account executive, argued that the costs were out of line, we had to move more quickly or the agency would be in the red on the campaign. So we ended up using models, old people who were professional old people in staged settings. The client was satisfied with the ads. The copy was strong and it looked as if Steven Robbins had done it again, but I knew what the ads could have been. If we had taken more time, they could have been terrific.

Sarah had a part in the high school production of *Guys and Dolls* but she knew better than to break into her parents' schedules. She told us that she had no lines in

the play and was only in the chorus—it was not necessary for us to attend. Beverly was busy that night with
a group show of local artists at the Institute. I had been
in Atlanta on business, but managed to make a late-
afternoon plane, and I went directly from the airport to
the high school, finding a seat in the back of the audito-
rium a few minutes after the show had begun. Sarah was
one of the Salvation Army girls. In the second act, I was
astonished to see that she had a solo. She sang "More I
Cannot Wish You," a touching performance of a lovely
song, and she stopped the show. After the play ended, I
startled her by greeting her in the backstage area.

"Sarah, you were so marvelous! Why didn't you tell
us?"

"It was sort of last minute. The boy who was supposed
to do it got sick. And they substituted a girl. And I got it."

"You should have said something to us!"

"Well—I didn't want to be disappointed when you
couldn't come."

A cable television station on Long Island presented a
program called "Lifestyles," an interview show with people who were considered to have interesting occupations.
They contacted Beverly and invited us to be guests. Beverly and I discussed it and decided this would be good
publicity for the Institute, and we agreed to appear. We
arrived at the studio for a Thursday-night program, the
producer, a woman in her thirties, said she was delighted
to have us and wanted to explore our particular lifestyle,
how we managed to make our marriage work given the
fact of two active careers.

"I hoped I could talk about my school," Beverly said.

"Oh, we'll do that, too," the producer answered.

The host was a writer in her late forties named Martha Wheeler. She used the word "wonderful" almost as a verbal pause. "We have as our guests tonight the most wonderful couple with a really wonderful lifestyle. She is Beverly Robbins who runs the wonderful—" and she checked her index card—"Nassau Institute of Children's Art, and her husband, Steven Robbins, president of the—" checking her card—"Robbins and Tolchin Advertising Agency. So, tell us—how do you manage to keep two wonderful careers going at the same time?"

Beverly glanced over at me and said:

"Steve is not a man who expects his wife to bring him his dinner every night on a silver tray. We try to be flexible, for neither of us to be sexist—if that word is still in use."

"Wonderful," the host said. Then she turned to me and asked: "How do you feel about your wife being so successful?"

"The important thing is for Bev to express herself. If she's happy doing that, then I'm happy and we're all happy."

"Wonderful. You have two—" checking her card— "daughters. How do they feel about all this? Beverly, are you always there to make dinner for them?"

"No one is really in charge of meals at our house. We all help."

"Does that include you, Steven?"

"Whenever I can."

The program lasted for twenty-seven minutes of air

time. It felt as though we were there overnight. There was something cheap about our posing, I could sense Beverly becoming uncomfortable about it as I was, the two of us putting on a performance for promotion purposes. I was asked a few questions about the advertising business: "How do you get your ideas?" "From real life," I answered, and the moderator said that was wonderful. Eventually, Beverly was able to discuss the Institute and talk about the programs she offered. The phone number for the Institute was shown on the screen, so from a publicity aspect, our first and last television appearance was useful. In closing, the moderator said:

"Beverly and Steven Robbins have a special relationship. They respect each other's careers, and the traditional husband and wife roles do not exist in their household. They just seem to—flow in and out, wouldn't you say, Beverly Robbins?"

"Yes, I suppose."

"Steven Robbins?"

"Yes. We flow. I flow one way and Beverly flows the other."

"Wonderful."

Chapter 9

B **EVERLY SUGGESTED THAT** we see a marriage counselor and I agreed. We needed help. Sylvia Pressman, a silver-haired woman of about fifty, was someone Beverly had met at several community functions. She had an office in her home in Glen Cove. In our first meeting, she asked Beverly and me to talk about our relationship so we could hear each other describe the situation. Both of us said that we were work-preoccupied, and that we had spent little time being attentive to one another. Sylvia was of the opinion that we did not have much of a life together as a couple and recommended that we see her on a regular basis. The discussion between husband and wife concerning a convenient hour for the sessions was in and of itself a reason to seek a marriage counselor.

We settled on ten o'clock Saturday mornings, and over the weeks that followed, Sylvia explored our personal psychologies, suggesting that I might not have had the best example in the world in my parents' marriage, while Beverly was confronted by the possibility that she might have been holding herself back from me to court her parents' approval. Sylvia also talked about an empty nest syndrome, that with the children older we no longer had them as a team goal to connect us. The psychological factors Sylvia presented seemed less persuasive to us than the realities of our daily lives, and we kept returning to the problems of two people in demanding careers. One day Sylvia said:

"What we have here are two people who still have concern for each other but haven't the time for the care a marriage requires."

"I don't know how you do it," Beverly said.

"There is no formula. You have to be attentive to each other's needs—and express those needs."

"If you need your head rubbed because you have a headache, it's hard to get your wife to rub it when *she* has a headache."

Sylvia looked perplexed.

"This is a new development, to have the woman working at the same level of intensity as the man. We don't know what it will all mean yet."

"Just what I always wanted to be," I said. "A new development."

We decided to terminate the therapy. To give the counseling its due, we were more aware of the problems we had in being intimate with each other, but we did not require the services of a marriage counselor to tell us that we were under pressure because of our careers. Sylvia had suggested we try to interfere with the patterns we had established with each other, so Beverly came into New York and met me for lunch a couple of times, and I went out to Long Island and met her for lunch, with disastrous results, we were both so tense about how much time it was costing us in the middle of the day. We joined a film series at Stony Brook, movies were an interest we had once shared, and it obliged us to spend Wednesday nights together. We were not always able to protect the time from emergencies at work.

We decided to take a trip without the children—to Antigua in the Caribbean—ten days and nine nights to save a marriage. On the evening of our arrival, the steel band played "Yellow Bird," the first of innumerable "Yellow Birds" we were to hear. We tried. Two people never tried so hard to be romantic. We made love in the shower to the aroma of mildew, we made love in the middle of the day to the rattling of the air conditioner, we made love at night trying to find the right instant. "Wait a minute. There's a mosquito in the room." With clenched teeth, we were going to have a good time, since so much was at stake. But by the eighth day, having sat on the beach, and having entered the dance contest, and looked at the coral from the glass-bottomed boat, and seen the historical site, and heard more "Yellow Birds" than I thought possible, we were bored with the tranquility of the tropics and ready to go back to the tensions that had produced the need to get away in the first place.

As we waited for the luggage at Kennedy Airport, we were both solemn, disappointed. We were tired from traveling but we did not go straight home from the airport, I drove aimlessly along secondary roads, hoping that one of us would think of something to say that could help. I parked on a dead-end street.

"I won't be Pat Cleary," she said suddenly.

"I wouldn't want you to be. A little, perhaps, but not really."

"Is this the price you have to pay? If you want to be independent, you get your marriage screwed up?"

"It's both of us. We're both so busy."

"I'm not running away from you, Steve. I'm just trying to do something on my own."

"I know. I love you, Bev."

"I love *you*. But I don't even know what that means. And I don't even know if it's enough."

Because of the problems in getting everyone together, I was given the choice of celebrating my forty-fifth birthday with a family dinner at an Italian restaurant two days early or one day late. I chose two days early to get it over with. I received a wallet from Beverly and slippers from the girls. I had received wallets and slippers, the gifts seemed as tired as I.

I was sitting in the living room reading a long memo from Tolchin concerning new accounts he wanted to solicit when Sarah breezed by on her way out for the evening. They came around several times a week, boys with expensive cars. They were once the enemy, boys as rich as these. Now they waited in the foyer for my daughter and called me "sir." Had I co-opted the enemy or had the enemy co-opted me?

We took on a new account, a health food company that was about to market a line of herbal teas on a national basis. I recommended a television-and-print campaign which stressed that caffeine was found in most teas, but not in these herbal teas. A nutritional chart was to be included in the print ads and the line I wrote for the campaign was: "The tea you can take before bed." The advertising manager of the company said, "You're a genius."

I had wanted desperately to succeed in the advertising field, an old battle that eventually I had won. Having won, I no longer had benefit of the quest. I was left with the work itself and after twenty years the work had become increasingly monotonous to me. I was obliged continually to turn out clever phrases here, gimmicks there.

One could do acceptable work and be bored at the same time, and this was disturbing to me—it seemed to prove how unimportant the work was in the first place. The public looked at what I had done, turned the page or flipped the dial, then bought the product or did not. I was called a "creative" executive, but my creations did not touch people in any significant way, my work was not anything the public cared about, nothing I did was of lasting value.

When I was younger, I had written a commercial with a batter hitting a plastic plate past a pitcher, now I had a ballet dancer dancing in ballet shoes made of a new paper towel, and another with an elephant sitting on a football helmet. I was repeating myself—and you don't bat plastic plates or dance in paper towels, elephants don't sit on football helmets. It was ridiculous, and yet, in advertising, it was considered very fine work.

I wrote a campaign for a new line of hi-fi speakers, the speakers were to be on the market for a year and then

the manufacturer was going to discontinue them for
another line. Hi-fi ads, tea commercials, they were different, the same. Everything I worked on was becoming
interchangeable to me. I went to meetings, constantly
doling out clever little ideas. I argued with Tolchin
about his headhunting for new accounts. And as my dis-
enchantment increased, I ate too much and drank too
much, writing off the excessiveness with credit cards,
coming back to the office from business lunches, sluggish
from the food and the wine.

One of our clients was Frederick Boujez, who had
changed his name from Fred Birnbaum when he took
over his family's business. He was in his late twenties,
five feet seven, dark, with good-looking features that he
liked to appraise in the reflection of mirrors and windows. Under his direction, Boujez Enterprises, formerly
Birnbaum Products, expanded from perfumed soaps to
a low-priced line of perfumes and colognes. Tolchin was
excited about the account, he thought it was "good diver-
sification" for the agency. I was having problems with
Boujez. He wanted to name a new perfume after a tough-
looking Broadway dancer he was seeing named Diedre
DeLuca.

"Trust me on this, Steve. She's gonna be another Lau-
ren Hutton."

"Diedre is hard to say. Why don't we do some market
testing?"

"Don't gimme a hard time. Just get me some layouts. I
already promised her a fragrance."

I asked the copy and art departments to start develop-
ing ideas, but when Boujez and I were having a business

lunch, he drank more than I and drunkenly told me that he was not really interested in creating a product, only in creating layouts, so he could use the material to keep the girl in his bed. I was already having dark thoughts about the monotony and the triviality of my work—now I felt like a pimp.

The problem was solved for me when the girl suddenly left town with her new lover, who happened to be a woman.

"There's a bottom line to it, Steve. I'm gonna turn the experience into profits."

Two weeks later, Boujez called for a meeting at the agency with my partner and me. Boujez arrived wearing his best custom-made suit and new Gucci shoes, so the meeting was to be Important.

"Homos are getting very big these days," he announced.

"Oh?" I said.

"I want to go after The Homo Market."

"The Homo Market?"

"Steve, I had some research done," and Boujez placed a folder in front of me prepared by our research department. It was evident that Tolchin had permitted this to be prepared without my knowledge. The report was entitled "The Homosexual Market in America." I leafed through it quickly. It contained various estimates of the numbers of homosexuals in market areas in the United States, projected buying power of homosexuals, a loathsome document.

"I've thought a lot about this. What homos need," Boujez said, "is their own fragrance! And we're gonna give it to them!"

I put my head in my hand to prop it up.

"Fred, we've been hearing about gay rights," I told him. "But I don't recall that as one of their demands."

"I want to introduce two new homo lines, one for men and one for women. I've already got the names—'Macho' for men and 'Lesbo' for women."

"Steve, this is your area, of course," Tolchin said. "But Fred and I were talking about ads which feature touching."

"And naked," Boujez added. "Naked and touching, that's the breakthrough."

"But tasteful," I said sarcastically.

"Steve, I'm counting on you to come up with brilliant copy for me, beautiful ads."

"This is very important to Fred," Tolchin said, coaching me. "He believes this is a milestone in American marketing."

"Let's see if I have this. You want to isolate homosexuals as a market and get them to walk into stores everywhere for a product that identifies them in public as homosexuals?"

"They protest, don't they?" Boujez said. "In big groups with banners?"

"For their rights, not their aromas."

"Steve—"

Tolchin ended the meeting quickly and shepherded me into my office. He told me the agency would lose the account if I did not cooperate, that I was guilty of prior censorship if I resisted at this stage of product development, and that at least twelve people would be let go if we lost the account, and how did that sit with me? I squeezed my fingers against the side of my head.

"I also have a headache from this," he said.

"I have more than a headache," I said. "I have what sounds like it should be a French general."

"What?"

"General Malaise."

I agreed to take the research report home with me to read over the weekend. My agency was addressing itself to "The Homosexual Market." Is this what I've become, I said to myself, a pimp *and* an exploiter?

I was in the house, reading the report, when Amy bounded past me wearing her latest button, "Save the Whales."

"Fuck the whales!" I said to myself, under my breath.

She stopped in her tracks.

"What did you say. Daddy?"

"I said, Fuck the whales. You're saving whales and I'm sinking into the sea."

"Oh, Daddy—don't be so ethnocentric."

They grow up to call you names that don't even make sense. I sat with "The Homosexual Market in America" and she went off to save whales.

Chapter 10

BOUJEZ WANTED TO proceed carefully with his marketing milestone, so I was given a reprieve on what my position would be. He was going to do further research. "We gotta talk to the homo on the street," he said.

I came back to the agency after another "creative" business lunch, having consumed more than my customary quota of wine, and was feeling so logy I fell asleep on the couch in my office.

"I'm drained," I told Beverly that night.

"You look tired."

"I thought when the girls are at camp we could go somewhere for a couple of weeks. Not the Caribbean. No more 'Yellow Birds.'"

She looked at me carefully and then she said:

"Steve, I'd like to spend the summer away from you."

"Bev—"

"I need some time to be by myself."

"Are we that far gone?"

"I just need a separate vacation, that's all. People take separate vacations."

"Not for a summer."

"I'd like to take a place in Montauk. The camp can run without me. And that's what I want."

"What you're asking for is a trial separation."

"Don't make it worse than it is. Twenty years, Steve. If nothing else, we're due for a little time apart."

"A summer?"

"We've done a lot of things in our life because of what you needed. This is what I need."

"Your needs have not been ignored around here."

"Look, we're not in a good place right now. I want to sort out who I am and who we are. It might turn out that this is good for us."

"Or it might not."

"Well, I'm going to do it."

I knew the tone and Beverly's resolve. There was nothing to negotiate.

"Will I get to see you?"

"I don't know. I haven't figured out the details."

I must have looked as hurt as I felt.

"It's not the end of the world," she said.

"Montauk? It's pretty far out."

We both managed to smile.

"Well, you're going to do it anyway," I said. "So take the time you want, goddammit. We got through consciousness-raising. I guess we can get through the summer."

"Thank you, darling."

"It's not like you announced you were having an affair."

I did not say that out of cunning, it had not occurred to me. I asked offhandedly:

"I mean, you're not having an affair, are you?"

Her face turned crimson.

"Bevvy! You are!"

"No."

"Bev—"

"Not exactly."

"What does that mean?"

"Something happened. But it was nothing."

"Christ! Bev?"

"It wasn't an affair, Steve. Not an affair."

The two of us were trembling.

"It was just—an episode."

"An episode?"

"An incident. It was nothing."

"Bev, I could have had women. They're all around. But I never did."

"Steve, why did you have to ask?"

"Is this why you want to get away? For episodes?"

"No."

"Oh, Bevvy—"

"Steve, remember when I first had the idea for the business? You didn't put it down, or put me down. You said, 'It's great.' You said, 'Do it.'" She took my hands in hers. "I owe you so much."

"I owe *you* so much."

"We married very young, didn't we?"

I pulled away.

"A summer apart," I said. "We're so chic."

We no longer had sex. I was too angry to touch her. It was necessary for me to go on an overnight trip to Boston for a trade show. I almost decided not to tell anyone I would be gone, feeling that I would not even be missed. I chose to let Sarah know so that someone would have a record of my whereabouts. I also told her that Beverly and I would be spending the summer apart.

"I figured something like that."

"We don't know what it all means yet," I said, stealing a line from the marriage counselor.

"I'm never going to get married," she said flatly. I was stunned by the coldness of her remark. I felt I had failed her.

"There are good parts. And there's you. Having you was a good part."

"You don't have to get married to have children."

"You did in my day."

"Well, maybe I'll get married. But when I'm older. Not before I'm thirty."

She was not so definite. We had not set such a terrible example, after all.

"It's just that marriage is so—inconvenient," she said.

I took the shuttle from LaGuardia Airport and the moment the plane was airborne I felt sexually liberated. Beverly had broken a code of honor with me, I was free to have sex with the person of my choice. The stewardess, a slim brunette, collected my ticket, and I thought about my chances of making it with her standing up in the washroom, protected from the passengers by the "Occupied" sign. My fantasies became rampant, a wild bird had been released. I walked to the back of the cabin and noticed three attractive women passengers on board, two businesswomen and a college student, any of whom I would have substituted for the stewardess. I never liked her anyway. I was blocked by other passengers. None of the women were sitting near me and I could not execute a proper pass leaning over people.

I had come to Boston for a hi-fi trade show, our account was previewing its new line of speakers, and I had arranged to stay at a hotel near the site of the show. I ordered dinner from room service and fell asleep after watching a movie on television. In the morning, I had breakfast in the hotel coffee shop, my waitress was an overweight girl in her early twenties with a pretty face, who bungled my order, brought me coffee instead of tea, and left the dish on the pickup counter so long the pancakes arrived cold. I left an excessive tip. This was to compensate for the fantasy that had engaged me during breakfast—bringing her up to my room, ordering room service to show her what hot pancakes were really like, and then screwing her until she moaned, "You are the best lover at the hi-fi trade show," or words along that line.

The show was set up for hi-fi fans and for trade people who were there to do business with one another. At nine in the morning, on the floor of the convention with the hot lights and the displays proclaiming "Buy me!" "Place an order!" "Better than ever . . ." the event seemed hysterical to me.

"I'm not in the mood for this," I said to a model at

a booth. She smiled a smile she must have practiced in a mirror and handed me a brochure on a new hi-fi turntable.

"Just what I needed," I said.

I went to my client's booth, which featured a series of magazine ads I had written. The ads tried to explain some of the technical features of the hi-fi speakers. They were enlarged to four feet by six feet and looked obscene to me in that size.

"Steve, you came! Don't they look great?"

The president of the company was Mal Peterson, an engineer in his fifties. He shook my hand frantically and started to talk to me about responses to the ads. My mind drifted. I was thinking about Beverly, I saw' her in bed with someone else, he was in her, and she was responding, rocking back and forth, her hands all over him, her hands on his ass—on his ass for Christ's sake—rocking, drawing him out, and out—Peterson's remarks about favorable dealer response were somewhat out of context. The hi-fi speakers were on display with "Thus Spake Zarathustra" playing, which seemed to be plugged right into the inside of my head. I excused myself, saying I was going to look at the competitors' booths, but I wandered, watching the female models, imagining how much better they would look if only they would wash off their stage makeup, which led me to imagine myself showering with them.

Somehow I got through a business lunch with Peterson and three members of his staff, they did most of the talking, then we went back to the trade show, where the line of speakers was being presented at a press conference. This was the responsibility of an outside public relations firm we had hired.

"It went well, didn't it?" the publicist said to me afterward. He was in his thirties, aggressive, he wanted my business.

"Yes, it all seems like a great success," I said.

The time was after five, Peterson was going to a business dinner with his sales people and a few dealers, I had discharged my responsibilities. I sank into a chair in the refreshment area and I saw him coming toward me. He was shouting my name, "Steve! Steve Robbins!" It was Liebowitz from the days in California.

"Steve, buddy! It must be fifteen years."

"How are you, Liebow?" I said, shaking his hand. "It's more like twenty."

"I saw your name so many times. I always meant to call you, but I just couldn't. You know, with you being such a big shot."

"Is that what I am?"

"You must be one of the top five creative minds in the advertising business today. I mean, the top five!"

Liebowitz and his hyperbole—

"What are you up to, Liebow?"

"I'm doing great. I own a mail-order business in Chicago. Anything you can think of, we ship. Giant balloons, stereos, electric toothbrushes. We're the biggest mail-order house west of the Alleghenies. The biggest."

"That's great."

"So tell me, you still married?"

"Yes." Technically correct, I thought. "I'm still married."

"I got married, I got divorced. I got married, I got divorced again. You with your wife?"

"No."

"So let me buy you dinner. And after, if you want, I'll get you laid, tiger, like always."

"Liebowitz, you never got me laid. And I don't think *you* were getting laid."

"You got to be kidding. I invented the matinee in the state of California."

"Liebowitz."

"Come on, Steve."

"Sure. Let's have dinner."

We went to a seafood restaurant near the convention hall, Liebowitz maintained a high level of sexual tension throughout, he flirted with waitresses, stared at women seated at other tables.

"They got to know you really want it. They love it when they know you're hungry for it."

I was at a point where I did not know whether to humor him or take it as good advice. He asked me to guess how many women he had had in his life. "Over two hundred," he said. I believed him. This seemed important enough to Liebowitz for him to have kept count and I wondered what it would have been like to have experienced over two hundred women. He regaled me with The Great Lays of History. "She was the best ever in Green Bay, Wisconsin." I might have begun to dismiss all this as bravado but he was making eye contact with a woman having dinner with a man a few tables away.

He excused himself, went to the men's room, she went to the ladies' room and he returned with her phone number, which she had given him on a piece of paper when they were out of view.

"I'm amazed, Liebow. I have the feeling something's been going on all the time that I just learned about."

"Communication. I'm in the communication business."

The woman left with a last glance in Liebowitz's direction and he leaned back in his chair, satisfied with himself.

After a while he went to a pay phone to call the date he had for this night and returned to tell me that he was sorry, but his friend did not have a friend for me. Just before we parted company, we exchanged business cards.

"Fantastic," he said, looking at mine. "I always knew you'd go places, Steve. You're some smart guy."

"I don't know anything, Liebow."

I returned to the hotel and tried to decide whether to take a plane back to New York or stay the night in Boston, deciding to stay, since I did not have a compelling reason to return home. I ordered a cognac from room service and turned on the television set. I was not ready to sleep and too keyed up to remain in the room. I took the elevator down to the hotel cocktail lounge. The place was noisy, the serious drinkers had settled in, another convention was in town, people with nameplates were gathered in various sized groups. A piano player was producing show tunes in a monotonous medley, making everything sound like "The Impossible Dream." I sat at the bar, ordered a stinger and watched the end of a Red Sox game on television. To my right was the only other drinker sitting at the bar, a man in his fifties, consuming scotch sours at a rapid pace. At eleven sharp, the man rose, said goodnight to the bartender, turned, and in an effortless motion, fell to the floor like a wooden plank. "My sentiments entirely," I said, as I tried to help him to his feet. The bartender and a waiter removed the man before he could offend any of the steadier drinkers in the room. A few minutes later a petite redhead in her thirties with an attractive but tired face and a sexy body sat in a stool to my left, accompanied by a stocky man in a leisure suit. I watched the news on television and looked at them in the bar mirror. I guessed that he was a hi-fi salesman about to cheat on his wife with the redhead. They had a disagreement and he walked out, leaving the redhead and me to stare at each other in the mirror. What would Liebowitz do at a time like this? I wondered. I produced a solitary drinker's chuckle at the notion that Liebowitz had become my role model.

"Is something funny?" she said.

"This and that." A truly dumb retort.

"Are you here for a convention?" she asked across the empty stool.

"Hi-fi."

"You're in hi-fi?"

"Advertising."

"Really?"

She moved her drink and her body toward me.

"What do you do in advertising?"

"I'm beginning to wonder myself."

"My name is Jean."

"Steve."

"Are you from around here?"

"New York."

"That's nice."

She was not doing much better than I.

"I'd like to know about you, Steve. Will you buy me a drink?"

"All right."

"In your room? I have an hour, sugar. Anything you can think of for an hour, I'd like to do with you. Anything."

She had made it convenient for me. All I had to do was decide if I wanted her and at what price. I could see something appropriate here—Boujez, Tolchin, Beverly, my marriage—I should have been picking up a prostitute at a bar and making it with her in a hotel.

"It's where I'm at," I said.

"What?"

"I'm game, Jean."

"I should tell you, everyone I like I ask to contribute to a favorite charity of my choosing."

"What do you consider a suitable contribution?"

"A hundred dollars."

"That's impossible."

"We could make it seventy-five dollars, but I would only be able to stay half the time."

"Seventy-five dollars would be a lot for irony."

"I beg your pardon."

"I really don't think so."

"Then I'll put it to you this way, lover. Fifty dollars. One time."

"Well, when you consider that I'm not just buying a hot time, but I'm making a protest—"

"Huh?"

"Okay." I said.

We went into the elevator and I caught a glimpse of the two of us in the distorted image of the elevator's mirror, a used-up woman and a used-up man. We did not pass anyone on the way to the room, the corridor was quiet, a corridor indistinct from the ones above and the ones below, my room the same as those above and those below. I entered the room with a prostitute and became one of the countless other men in hotel rooms having seedy liaisons with women they did not know. Nobody had seen me, nobody would see me, I was anonymous. This, more than anything, appealed to me now. I had become exhausted with myself, and here in this place, I was no one—"Steve"—not even a last name.

In the bar she had said she wanted to know about me, but apparently she had decided to give conversation a lower priority. She began to remove my clothes, to kiss me on the neck and rub her hands along my thighs. We undressed each other and settled down on the bed. Her skin was rougher than Beverly's, her breasts larger, her nipples darker. I seized these sensations, grabbing at her, kissing her all over, and when I entered her, I pushed hard and as she wrapped her legs around me and pressed herself up toward me, I was thinking of Beverly for an instant—and then I wondered how I was in bed. I had no sense of this, twenty years of making love only to your wife. My mind was racing. It was a very busy performance. I tried to hold myself off, make the fifty dollars last, I said to myself, and the sheer weight of the money worked as a strategy to delay orgasm for a moment or two.

She allowed us a few minutes of repose and then she got up from the bed and dressed very crisply. I reached for my wallet and discovered I only had thirty dollars.

"I'm short cash."

"I'm not on Master Charge, sugar."

"I have traveler's checks."

"We don't cash traveler's checks."

"I mean I'll cash them downstairs. Why don't you just wait?"

She was skeptical.

"I'm not skipping out. I've got a suit here and my luggage."

I put on slacks and a shirt, slipped on my shoes and left a prostitute in my room, with my suit as security, so I could cash in a traveler's check to pay her, which I thought was the perfect touch. I returned, gave her the money, and she asked if I wanted her phone number. I considered this a form of compliment, within limits, and I accepted her number, permitting her to rise from bar hooker to call girl.

"There is a certain quaintness to the ritual," I said.

"What?"

"See you around, Jean."

"Any time."

Beverly had her episode and now I had one, too. That did not mean I could sleep. I checked out of the hotel and sat in a waiting area at Logan Airport, staring dully ahead, "One of the top five creative minds in the business." Of the aspirations I had for myself when I was younger, I had achieved everything. And in the glaring light of an airlines terminal in the middle of the night I was exposed for who I had become, a sagging, burned-out middle-aged man with a troubled marriage, who could have just sat there or boarded a plane going anywhere.

At about six in the morning, I got out of the chair where I had been sitting for hours, went into the men's room and vomited up the bile of myself and of this night, as the Muzak played cheerfully, idiotically, above me.

Chapter 11

MY NEW YORK-TO-BOSTON sexual fantasies gave way to Boston-to-New York revenge fantasies. The plane would crash, I would be dead—so there. Beverly would grieve and feel guilty and perhaps I might mess up a couple of New Year's Eves for her.

"Have a nice day," the stewardess was intoning when we landed.

"I guess we made it," I said. She could deal with strange, red-eyed passengers in the morning. They had training schools for that. She just looked at me and said, "Have a nice day."

I went straight to the agency, needing a shave, my clothes wrinkled.

"I want us to resign the Boujez account," I said to Tolchin in his office.

"First of all you look like shit. And second, you're nuts," he said, succinctly.

"It's cheap and exploitative and beneath us."

"Anything else?"

"I'm just not in the business of doing that kind of work."

"So don't. You've got staff here. Someone else can work on it."

"Macho and Lesbo. What are we, Ray?"

"Business people."

"Let someone else do his advertising."

"We can't afford it."

I felt trapped, nauseous. I tried to open the window, but we were in one of those modern office buildings with windows you are discouraged from opening. I tried to bang it open to get air. I kept banging. The stuck window and my general frustration came together and I was just standing there, pounding on the goddamn window that would not open, pounding, pounding.

Tolchin grabbed me and spun me around.

"Are you cracking up?"

"Goddamn window!"

"We can't resign Boujez. It'll cost us a fortune."

"We'll drink less at lunch."

"Steve, it's only a concept. They don't even have the products yet."

"Macho and Lesbo."

"It could fall through. There's nothing we have to do right now. We don't have to resign the account."

I had stopped listening to him. I was looking out the window. We had a good view from our offices, high up. From Tolchin's corner office and from mine we could see north and south on Madison Avenue. If I jumped out the window I would certainly raise the guilt potential of my death. But of course I could not commit suicide there. I could not get the goddamn window open.

"Steve, where are you?"

"We've got good views. Good views, good suits, good desks."

"Steve—"

I turned toward him.

"You give out little pieces of yourself and it comes back in the form of good suits and good desks."

"I think you need a rest, Steve. I think you should stay away from the office for a while."

"You're probably right," I said, and I looked around the room. "I've lost the theme."

I told Beverly I would be working at home for a few days and I made work for myself, I read books and back issues of magazines. My presence in the house seemed to be of little concern to my family, Beverly was trying to conclude matters so she could get away for her summer, Sarah was going through a series of end-of-high-school parties, Amy was attending meetings on the end of the world.

Beverly and I appeared as a normal couple for Sarah's graduation from high school. She would be entering Vassar in the fall. We went to lunch at the Russian Tea Room in New York. Either Beverly or I could have paid the check with any of the four credit cards we had between us. We had two children, four credit cards, and three checking accounts, one joint account, and both Beverly and I had individual personal checking accounts, neither of us trusting the other's bookkeeping. I never knew if that had been a sign of the liberated nature of the relationship or a sign of its hopelessness.

We had a last social function to perform together before the separation began. Pat Cleary had invited us to a surprise birthday party for John, and as a courtesy to Pat we agreed to attend. We dressed silently, we had little to say to each other these days, Beverly donning her layers of Calvin Klein, I in my ever-present good suit. As we stood before the full-length mirror in our bedroom, I said:

"A terrific-looking couple. Who would know?"

"Try not to drink too much tonight."

"Do you still have the right to ask me that?"

"I thought I did."

The Clearys' house was dark, we rang the doorbell, Pat Cleary opened the door, the lights came on, people yelled, "Surprise!" a combo began to play "The Anniversary Song" and we walked into a surprise party for *us,* for our twentieth anniversary.

"Marzel Tov!" a voice cut through the noise. A beaming George, followed by a beaming Cindy, broke out of the crowd to embrace Beverly and shake hands with me. Sarah and Amy were there, the Clearys, Beverly's office staff with spouses and dates, neighbors, in all, thirty people were assembled to pay homage to the happy couple. The anniversary was a few days off. We had never bothered to discuss it.

"Surprised?" George asked.

"The look on their faces—" Cindy said, smiling.

"It was Grandma's idea," Sarah told us privately. "We said you might not want it, but they insisted. We gave them the Clearys' number and they called them and everything." A three-piece combo launched into a medley of twenty-year-old songs.

"They're the same songs from your wedding," Cindy said triumphantly. "I kept a list."

"I think I'm going to pass out. Or I'd like to," Beverly whispered in my ear.

"Me first."

"I take it back. Drink as much as you want."

We worked the room, smiling, accepting congratulations, until we had covered everyone. We picked up glasses of champagne from a waiter hired for the event, went into a bedroom and closed the door. We looked at each other and could not keep from laughing.

"Your parents—they're crazy. I mean, *mashurgeh.*"

"I know. This is the worst, most inappropriate—"

"I bet your father *knew* we were having trouble. He's taking some perverse pleasure from this."

"Maybe not. They are pretty corny. My mother—*the same songs.*"

"It's a wonder they didn't bring the horses."

We laughed again and then we stopped. We were experiencing too much pain.

The children went off to be counselors at camp, and on the day they left, Beverly loaded our station wagon to move out of the house for the summer. I leaned against the side of the house and watched her carry her clothes to the car.

"Something in me objects to helping you so you can leave me."

"I'm not leaving you."

"Right. It's a separate vacation. I'll use that, if anybody asks."

I watched her struggle with her suitcase and then I came forward to help carry it into the car.

"I hope that counts for me. On some cold, rainy night— you left behind a man who helps with a suitcase."

"Steve, this is not a happy moment for me. It's just something 1 have to do."

"Do I get your phone number? What if I die?"

"If you die, you won't need to call me."

She got into the car and rolled down the window.

"I'll be listed, Steve."

"I hate this," I said.

She pulled my head down and kissed me on the forehead. She was on the verge of tears, but she took on her resolute look, started the car and drove away.

I was alone. It intrigued me to realize that it was possible for me to die in this house and nobody would know until Labor Day. Thoughts of suicide occupied me, a fascinating subject, suicide, which I proceeded to convert into a research project. I went to the library and brought home several volumes on suicide. I imagined what it would be like to teach a course on suicide, Suicide 101, the history of suicide, types of suicides, suicide heroes and heroines, the course culminating in my own suicide, a memorable course they would talk about for years. After alternately amusing and depressing myself, I thought about one theory I had read that had particular force for me—the idea that in suicide a person can feel, for a brief moment, that he has gained control of his life by controlling the time and manner of his death. This interested me, with my life feeling as if it were skittering out of my control. I had no focus. I had no interest in going to work. I had no family life now. I stopped shaving, bathing, I rose in the morning in my pajamas and stayed in them all day. I watched television, soap operas, game shows. "I am not suicidal," I announced to myself one day while watching a soap opera. "I want to know how these people make out." Then I laughed out loud, uncertain if I had been talking out loud as well. I did not know if I had been walking around the house, saying aloud the thoughts that were in my head, and then I decided it did not matter anyway, since no one could see me or hear me. I ate the food that had been left in the kitchen, dinners of Product 19 and beer, eventually calling in an order that was delivered, frozen pizzas, canned soups, more beer. I watched movies late into the night, going to sleep at three or four in the morning. When I awoke I was still tired, so I began to take naps, sometimes twice a day. I established a cycle: late night, tired in the morning, nap. Unable to sleep at night because of nap in the day, late night, tired in the morning, nap. The naps became a form of narcotic. They left me feeling less than fully awake all day, with heavy eyes, my mind and body deadened to sensation.

My secretary called every morning at eleven, wondering when I would be back, often waking me. I remembered the standard excuse from school days, "Steven was out with an upset stomach."

"I am out with an upset stomach," I told her one morning.

"When do you think you'll be back?" she inquired a few days later.

"I don't know."

"The mail, the memos—they keep piling up. Should I get them to you?"

"Give it all to Mr. Tolchin," I said. "He has the stomach for it."

She kept calling, I told her my stomach was better and I was now taking a vacation. After a week, ten days, two weeks, I cannot be certain, she called to say that Tolchin was out of town and there was a layout that needed my approval.

"I've decided to take a leave of absence," I told her. "I have no idea when I'll be back in the office."

"Oh, I see—"

"Please tell Mr. Tolchin."

"Of course, Mr. Robbins. But we do need an okay on this—"

"And now for five hundred dollars—" the game-show host was saying—"who was Peter Rabbit's cousin?"

"Benjamin Bunny," I said to my secretary.

"I beg your pardon."

"What is it, Miss Crawford?"

"Your okay? Could I send a messenger to the house?"

"I don't care."

"Thank you, Mr. Robbins."

"I'd appreciate your not calling me here anymore, Miss Crawford."

"I'm sorry, Mr. Robbins."

"It's distracting."

I was thinking that I would have won that five hundred dollars, easy—if I had been on that show.

I began to do my Nat King Cole impersonations. I wondered if I could have made my living doing that, the way people do Al Jolson. I could have appeared on talk shows, chatted with the hosts, done a little "Walkin' My Baby Back Home." No, what I really should have been was an English professor at a small midwestern college. If only I had been a liberal arts major. That was where I made my mistake. I called my father in Florida.

"How are you, Dad?"

"Fine, Steve. You?"

"Great. Never better."

At the time I was standing in the kitchen in my pajamas at four in the afternoon with days of dishes in the sink.

"Dad, why I called—"

I took a mug that had cold tea in it, emptied the tea and poured scotch into the mug.

"What if I had said I wanted to be a liberal arts major?"

"Now?"

"Not now. When I was younger. If I said I wanted liberal arts—"

"Liberal arts? What would you do with liberal arts?"

"That's what I remembered. Thanks a lot, Dad. Speak to you soon."

"Be my love . . ." My Mario Lanza was way off. Your eyesight and your Mario Lanzas deteriorate with age. I began reading books in the house that I had always meant to read, but since my concentration was limited, I read for a while and then stopped, going on to the next unread book, leaving it unread. The doorbell rang. I did not know who it might be. The Avon Lady? If it were the Avon Lady, I would buy soap. I needed soap. I had not showered because I was out of soap, also showering would have been such an effort—I would have had to take my pajamas off and then put them on again.

"Robbins? Messenger."

He was a short, muscular man in motorcycle gear. His motorcycle was parked in the driveway. I opened the door for him.

"If you're the messenger, I must be Garcia."

"No, this is for Robbins."

"Yes, this is Robbins. Come in."

He gave me a manila envelope and followed me in as I sat down on the living room couch in my pajamas. The blinds were drawn, the living room floor was strewn with cups, drink glasses, magazines, books. I opened the envelope, glanced at a layout—it looked all right to me—took a pencil from an end table, initialed the layout, put it back in the envelope and handed it to him.

He was dumbfounded. He had traveled by motorcycle from New York City to an unshaven man in pajamas on Long Island who initialed a paper in seven seconds.

"That's it?" he said.

"That's what we do here."

He put on his helmet and started to leave, looking around, trying to take it all in. It was "Star Wars Meets the Collier Brothers." At least I gave him something to think about on his ride back.

In the basement I found the trunk with my old possessions. I looked at my Dixie Cup collection, my picture of George "Snuffy" Stirnweiss, my varsity jacket. I began to think about the old days, and the girls I had known, Carol Ershowsky, Fanny Pleshette, Carla Friedman. Would my life have been different if I had married one of them? I doubted it. Carla Friedman was a bookish type. Possibly she would have exerted an intellectual influence over me. All that would have changed was that I would have ended up teaching advertising rather than doing it. I had no excuses. I could not say, "The cat ate my homework." I got exactly what I thought I wanted.

Fanny Pleshette. Of all the girls it was Fanny Pleshette who stood out, the best one I did not marry. She did not mind that I had little money. She took me to her apartment in a house with a doorman and we made love. Fanny. I decided I would find out how she was doing. I called Barnard College to see if they had a record of a Fanny Pleshette through the alumni office. They did not, nobody was able to help me. I tried the Manhattan telephone book on the chance that she was still in New York and had not married or was using her maiden name. She was not listed, but a "J. Pleshette" was in the book and I recalled it as being her mother's address. I dialed the number.

"Hello, is this Mrs. Pleshette?"

"Who is this?"

"Excuse me, but my name is Steven Robbins. And many years ago I was a friend of your daughter's."

"Yes?"

"I guess you wouldn't remember me. Stevie Robbins. I went to City College. She was at Barnard at the time."

"I don't remember."

"Well, I got to thinking about old times and I was thinking about Fanny. Kind thoughts. And I wondered where she was, what she had done, and frankly, if I might be able to reach her."

"Fanny is dead, young man."

"Oh, no."

"She's dead."

"I'm so sorry."

"She died in 1970. She was killed in an automobile accident on the New York Thruway. She was with a man. They were planning to be married. A truck crossed into her lane. He was just bruised. She died instantly, I'm told."

"I am so, so sorry."

"She worked for the UN. She was a nice girl, wasn't she, my Fanny?"

"She was a wonderful girl."

"Well—goodbye now—what was your name?"

"Steven Robbins."

"I'm afraid I don't remember you."

I hung up the phone and I began to cry. Fanny. She would have been in her thirties when she died. She had gone on to live a life nearly as long after I had known her as she had lived when I had known her. Yet in my mind, she had never grown older. The person I wept for was a young girl who had died.

Chapter 12

THE PAST TOOK over the present. I could not remember what I had eaten for dinner the previous day or whether I had eaten at all, but I was remembering dinners of thirty years before. I sat in a chair, reliving my life, isolating the embarrassments, rejoicing in the good parts. It was better before.

I remembered how I could drive down the right side dribbling the ball away from the defender who would think I was too far into the corner, but there was still enough rim if I shot just before I went off the court at the end line, and I would let it go just as I was heading out of bounds, a soft, arching one-handed push shot. I would be off the court behind the basket by the time the ball dropped through, a flashy move, but a solid move. I was good out of that right corner. I was good all around the key. Nobody I knew, not John Cleary, not Ray Tolchin, not the Meltzers down the road, nobody could have outshot me with a running one-hander. John Cleary—I would have locked up John Cleary in ten seconds. All of them—they all would have fouled out trying to guard me.

In my senior year, De Witt Clinton was to play a big game against Taft High School. We were not going into the playoffs, but we could be spoilers and eliminate Taft in the last game of our season. My father arranged his schedule so he could come, the one time he saw me play in a game. The wooden stands were full, people sat along a running track above the court, legs dangling down, heads poking through the railings. I scored 36 points in that game, including the off-the-court push shot, two tip-ins, I stole three balls on defense and went in for layups, at one point I made six straight from the field, and I shut off the opposing forward with seven points. It was a performance noted by Sam the Man, who was in the stands and who gave me a "Great shooting, kid" outside the candy store that night. When the game was over and we had upset Taft 63-60, I ran off the court, sweating, beaming, surrounded by other players and by friends who pushed in to slap me on the back, and fighting through the crowd was my father. He hugged me awkwardly and I looked up and realized that my father who rarely registered feelings had tears in his eyes. "You're a fine boy, Stevie," he said. And then the moment was swept away by people, by strangers.

I played the game again. I was hugged by my father again.

I no longer knew the day of the week. I replayed stickball games. I had my fingers inside assorted bras and panties. I was soul-kissing Carla Friedman. I could have had her before I went to California. Memory taunted me.

I wanted all of an experience that was good, an entire walk through the neighborhood with Arthur and Jerry, every word said, every nuance, an entire Saturday night date in the Bronx, everything that happened, every part of the physical sensations—the hot fudge sundae at Krum's Soda Parlor, the warmth of Cynthia Cohen's crotch as I forced my hand underneath the crinoline beneath her skirt and tried to work my fingers below her moist panties. I could only summon fragments. I worked at it until I was mentally weary. I wanted more than fleeting images, I wanted to hold on to an entire experience, to have all of the good parts from the time when it was better. And in July, for the first time in weeks, I shaved, showered and dressed in clean clothes, and then I set out for the Bronx. My purpose was to buy a hot fudge sundae at Krum's. I called for a cab to take me to the railroad station. Instinctively, I knew that I should not trust myself to drive.

The train arrived at Penn Station and I went into the subway to go north to the Bronx. A newsstand dealer gave me directions, and I transferred at 59th Street from the A train to the D. As the train rocked back and forth on the stretch to 125th Street, I remembered that rocking. Coming home on a date sometimes it rocked you into an erection, and you had to put your hands in your pockets for camouflage. 145th Street. That was the stop for Lewisohn Stadium and the summer concerts. 155th Street. The old Polo Grounds. I saw Stan Musial play there and Mel Ott. 161st Street, still the Yankee Stadium. In a game against the Red Sox, DiMaggio hit a line drive into the right field corner and the throw from the outfield beat DiMaggio to the bag, but when Doerr put down the tag, Joe D. was not there. With a sweeping slide he slipped his toe into the bag and was safe at second, a great hitter, a wonderful fielder, but you had to remember what a fine base runner he was. I wanted to say that to the man sleeping next to me on the train. 167th Street. Jeannie Drago, the biggest breasts of anyone in my entire dating career, untouched by human hands. 182nd-183rd Streets. The Ascot Theater and Carla Friedman who let me feel her up beneath our coats which we huddled under during *Fanfan the Tulip* with Gerard Philipe. The train arrived at Fordham Road, the site of Krum's Soda Parlor.

When I stepped out onto the street I became dizzy with the flood of memories. The physical landscape was essentially as it had been twenty years before. The overall look was shabbier, somewhat dirtier, but nothing had been torn down, nor had any new buildings been constructed. Alexander's Department Store was there on Fordham Road, and the Dollar Savings Bank Building, and the Wagner Building to which my father had reported for civilian defense duty during World War II. Where stores had been located, stores existed. On 188th Street and the Grand Concourse, the place I now stood, Bickford's Cafeteria, the seltzer stop for the local horseplayers, was out of business. With appropriateness the location had been taken over by an off-track betting parlor.

I saw the sign on the other side of the street for Krum's but when I entered I found that it was no longer a soda parlor, it was a candy and card shop.

"Where is the ice cream?" I asked a young woman behind the counter.

"We don't sell ice cream."

"You don't sell ice cream? You should be ashamed of yourself."

I went back across the street to a candy store near the off-track betting parlor. A heavyset man in his fifties was behind the counter.

"A hot fudge sundae with chocolate ice cream, please."

"I'm out of hot fudge."

"How can you be out of hot fudge?"

"Easy. You open the tin and there's no hot fudge."

"Then I'll have a chocolate frappe."

"A what?"

"A chocolate frappe."

"I haven't heard anyone say frappe in years. What's a frappe?"

"It's syrup over ice cream."

"You want a sundae. Why don't you say a sundae?"

"If I wanted a sundae, I'd say a sundae. A sundae is whipped cream, it's nuts, it's a cherry. A frappe is just syrup."

"By me it's a sundae."

"By me it's a frappe."

"Listen, Mister, I'll give you a frappe. I'll give you a bromo. What the hell do I care?"

"I've come home," I said.

I walked north along the Grand Concourse and crossed Fordham Road, which was busy with shoppers. The people were mostly Hispanics and blacks. Looking east and west along Fordham Road I could see that it was still thriving with retail stores. Just north of Fordham Road, Sutter's Bakery was in its old location on the Grand Concourse. I had been dispatched there for a coffee ring on many a weekend morning, my parents were lucky if the cake arrived home with the pecans. I bought half of a coffee ring on this day and began to devour it outside the bakery. An old woman observing smiled at me.

"Good?" she said.

"Good. Do you want a piece?"

"No, thank you. Enjoy."

"I am."

I continued along the Grand Concourse, walking slowly, trying to absorb the sensations, worried that I was about to come upon a row of condemned buildings, burnt mattresses in the street, cars abandoned and stripped—my childhood neighborhood desecrated. But this section of the Bronx, north of Fordham Boad near Kingsbridge Boad, was not blighted. I reached Poe Park, it seemed the neighborhood was still predominantly Irish Catholic and Jewish. In the park, young mothers sat on benches as their children played, some of the old people were involved in shuffleboard games or were playing cards and checkers. I searched for a familiar face. I recognized no one. At the end of the park, still standing, was Poe Cottage, a farmhouse where Edgar Allan Poe had lived. I had first visited it with class 1-1 of P.S. 86, nearly forty years before.

I took a deep breath anticipating what I was to do next. I crossed to the west side of the street and walked down the hill of Kingsbridge Road and entered my old neighborhood. On both sides of the street the stores were fully rented. The Fishers were gone from the candy store, and the Rosens were gone, but it was still a functioning neighborhood, drugstore, fish store, kosher butcher, coffee shop, pizza store, shoppers were on the streets, cars and buses were moving along. Kingsbridge Road was virtually as it had been when I left. I looked at the side streets, the red brick buildings had become murky with age, the white brick buildings had yellowed, but these apartment houses were occupied, sheet metal did not cover windows, garbage was not scattered through the streets as in the photos I had seen of the South Bronx. I stopped in front of Beatrice Arms and I shuddered from the impact of seeing the building again.

I looked up at the window where my mother had tossed down shopping money wrapped in a handkerchief.

I stood in the vestibule checking the names on the bells. I did not know anyone. The entrance door was locked and I waited for someone to come along. A little boy walked out and I went inside, the flamingo wallpaper was gone, the walls were green, the elevator door with the art deco nymphs was now painted with black enamel. I took the elevator to the third floor and stood outside my childhood apartment. I rang the bell and a peephole opened in the door.

"My name is Robbins," I called out. "I used to live in this apartment. I was wondering if I could come in."

The door opened several inches, held in place by a chain.

"Are you a burglar?" a man's voice asked.

"I really used to live here. About twenty years ago.

Next door was a Mrs. Corrigan. Could I look around, just for memories?"

The door opened and a man in his twenties, taller than I, sturdy-looking, was standing there.

"You better not be a burglar."

"I just want to look at where I lived. I appreciate this."

The floors, which had been bare, were now covered by carpeting, a modern bedroom set was placed in what had been my parents' room, the living room and my bedroom were reversed. Our living room was a children's bedroom with bunk beds, my bedroom was their living room.

"It's a little bit turned around. I used to sleep in there."

I walked into my old room and I looked out the window. I used to watch from there to see if any stickball games were under way. Jerry and Arthur would stand below and call up to me. I stepped away from the window and rested my forehead against the wall.

"You okay, Mister?" the man asked.

"No."

I turned to him.

"I used to be very happy in this room."

"Can I get you a drink of water or something?"

"Please. Bronx water."

He gave me a glass of water and I drank it down.

"This was a good neighborhood," I said.

"It's still pretty good, compared to some places."

"You have children?" I asked.

"Two boys. My wife is a teacher. I'm a police officer."

"Then it's lucky for me I'm not a burglar."

Years before, I had made a tiny drawing with India ink and a pen in a secret place, just above the molding in the bottom of the bedroom closet. "Stevie was here," I had drawn, in the style of "Kilroy was here."

"This may look odd," I said to the man as I got on my knees and searched in the bottom of the closet. It was still there, missed by house painters over the years, "Stevie was here."

After I left the apartment, I wandered through the neighborhood, past the Kingsbridge Armory, P.S. 86, then along the Jerome Park reservoir and the campus of what had been Hunter College and was now called Lehman College. I stopped at the sandlot diamonds at Harris Field. A few joggers were running the route along the reservoir. I did not think I was capable of running twenty yards.

I walked back to Kingsbridge Road, the neighborhood was busy with street life, teenagers were gathered in front of the pizza store, people were walking dogs, the stores were busy with shoppers. Even on a warm summer day the pulse was more active than anything I had known in the suburbs. I took the subway and returned to Great Neck by train.

I was back the next day. And the next. And the next. I kept coming back. I rose each day to an alarm clock, showered, shaved, dressed in clean clothes and made the trip to the Bronx. After a while I trusted myself to drive. I went to sleep early and awoke each morning with a purpose. Going back had become my reason for being. I strolled with the strollers. I leaned against cars. I bought sandwiches and ate on park benches. I watched card games played by old men in Poe Park. I sat silently at the end of dark Irish bars drinking beer in the middle of afternoons. I peered through the fence looking at teenagers play basketball. I haunted my old neighborhood like a restless ghost.

Chapter 13

THE FISHERS' CANDY store was now run by a man named Chris Anton, who had attempted to modernize the place with a new Formica counter and a griddle for fast-food items, a candy store owner with delusions of luncheonettes. The aroma was gone, that special smell created by spearmint leaves, jujubes and assorted ecstasies.

"Do you sell loose candy?" I had asked him.

"It's not worth it," he said. He was in his early fifties, a pudgy, sad-faced man.

"Could I have an egg cream?"

He made it with too much syrup, too little milk, too much foam. The man did not know what he was doing.

"How much?" I asked.

"Forty cents."

"I used to work here. An egg cream was six cents."

"It costs me six cents to wash the glass," he said somberly.

The store was on the south side of Kingsbridge Road,

a few doors east of Jerome Avenue. I stopped in regularly for sodas and sandwiches, and Chris Anton began to feel free enough to complain to me. Costs were high, he had to compete with the pizza store, the coffee shop and a McDonald's. I did not view the McDonald's which had opened on Jerome Avenue as a sign of the neighborhood's vitality, but as an invasion of suburbia. I sympathized with Chris, a man who was like Joe Btsfplk from the old Li'l Abner comic strip, a character with a perpetual rain cloud over his head.

Occasionally I would see a face in the neighborhood that looked familiar, but after twenty years of being away from here, the people I had known were gone. I strolled to other neighborhoods, the Ascot Theater, home of *Open City* and the *Fanny* trilogy had met with tragedy in my view. It was a porno house. Walking farther south along the Grand Concourse, it appeared at first that the area was not blighted, but when I went only one or two blocks east or west of the Grand Concourse it was like stepping off a cliff, neighborhoods were sliding into filth and neglect. Compared to these neighborhoods, mine had been spared, whites, Hispanics and blacks had managed a kind of balance between them, landlords had not abandoned buildings, the city agencies had not neglected services. The place where I had grown up was holding on, my roots had not been obliterated.

One morning I parked near St. James Park, opened the trunk of the car and removed a newly purchased basketball. Wearing a T-shirt, dungarees and sneakers, I walked to a vacant basketball court, my first time on a court in years, and with the move I had imagined, dribbled down the right side for my drifting off-the-court push shot. I felt a stabbing pain in my shoulder and I missed the rim by two feet.

I tossed the ball a few inches above my head, catching it and flipping it up again, getting a sense of the grain and the weight of the ball against my fingertips. I dribbled slowly to the basket and carefully laid it up and in. A beginning. I shot baskets for an hour, never quite making that drifting push shot, and then sat with my back against a fence, exhausted. Several teenage boys came by, shooting baskets, jocking around. "Wanna play?" one of them called out to me. I shook my head, no. That would have been a new category of suicide—Suicide by Schoolyard Basketball.

I went to the candy store for an egg cream. Chris Anton made a flat, murky drink for me.

"Chris, this is a sophisticated drink. It's for the candy store connoisseur."

"I know I've been doing it wrong," he said, mournfully. "Why don't you show me?"

I came behind the counter and made the drink as he watched, trying to add old soda jerk's flourish, diverting the seltzer off the spoon into the glass. Along with my push shot, another misplaced move. I managed to get seltzer all over my shirt.

After nearly two more hours of shooting baskets, I drove back to Long Island, took a hot bath and got into bed. The following morning I had difficulty lifting my arm to brush my teeth. I intended to go back to the Bronx, but the way my body ached I did not think I could manage to drive. Wearing my T-shirt, dungarees and sneakers, and carrying my basketball, I boarded the Long Island Railroad train to New York, oblivious to the way I looked to the commuters in their shirts and ties.

By the time I reached New York and went into the subway, I was absorbed by the city's activity. In New York, the sight of a middle-aged man carrying a basketball did not warrant any particular attention. I arrived in the Bronx, walked into the park and started to shoot baskets. I had a specific goal now. I wanted to be able to play in a three-man basketball game with the local kids and still be alive when it was over. To accomplish this, I intended to follow a program of shooting baskets and jogging. My jogging goal was to run around the reservoir near Kingsbridge Road, a mile and a half without stopping, and also without dying.

At the reservoir I started to run ten strides, then walk ten strides, which had been recommended in a jogging book. The book did not include material on resting against the fence. I did a considerable amount of resting against the fence and managed to cover the distance in about forty minutes or a day, I was too tired to tell. Plan A of my program called for another hour of shooting baskets and stretching exercises. I created Plan B, the suspension of activities, the returning to Long Island and the getting into bed. I set the alarm before I went to sleep, and when it rang in the morning, I could not reach up and over for it, I moved my arm a few inches and pulled the plug out of the wall. Plan C. I stayed in bed with a heating pad.

After resting a day, I returned to the reservoir and I started myself off with an "Oh, shit!" I was going to lose that paunch, which I hated. I was gagging for breath, but

I was going to get myself into shape. I went to the basketball court and shot baskets with aching arms until I could not lift the ball any longer. I came back every day for two weeks, jogging, doing stretching exercises and shooting baskets. I finally made it around the reservoir at a steady gait. Children passed me, obese women, but I finished.

I infiltrated the teenagers' game with a standard schoolyard approach, territorial aggression. While they were practicing, I brought my ball over and began shooting baskets at their court. "You playing?" someone asked when six people were on the court. I nodded. "Okay, you got this guy," he said. I was not even in the game and I was already traded.

They were high school age, one of them at six feet two was two inches taller than I, the others were assorted heights, the smallest about five feet six. Two were blacks, two Hispanic, one white. They played fast basketball with more physical contact and less team play than I remembered from my days of schoolyard ball. Everyone on the court considered himself a shooter and they were gunning sloppily from all over the court. My reflexes were terrible. I had been practicing shots, I had not been playing, and it took several ball games for me to find a rhythm, but it did not matter—I was lost on the court. I set people up with passes, they did not know how to move without the ball, they only knew how to dribble and shoot, and my passes went out of bounds. I looked for the ball when my teammates were out of position and I was free for a shot, and watched as they took wild jump shots. I stayed there for about two hours as players drifted on and off, I waited for the next game when the team I played with lost, but in every case, whoever won, the result was the same. I was out of the game. That night I sat in my house on Long Island and analyzed schoolyard basketball games as they were played in the Bronx. I was All-Neighborhood once. I had to be able to compete with these kids. The next day I arrived with a game plan. My high school coach had taught defense to us, playing defense was one of the differences between the average schoolyard ballplayer and someone who had been coached. If I maintained my concentration, I thought I might be able to assert myself with these ballplayers through defense. I started to anticipate, knock the ball away and pick off passes. I became more confident and was slowly becoming a factor on the court. On offense I wanted the ball now, I was as entitled to shoot as they were, and I made a few baskets. In my sixth game, a mad jump shooter named Juan tried the same predictable move three times in a row and I knocked the ball out of his hands each time. The last time, the tips of my fingers lightly grazed his shirt.

"Foul, you mother!" he shouted. "This mother's been foulin' me all day."

"You're full of it," I said.

"Oh, yeah?"

"Oh, yeah! You didn't look like you dunked it to me."

The others on the court supported me, laughing.

"Forget it, Juan," one of them said. "This guy put you in a box."

Juan took the ball and slammed it against the back-board and walked off the court. The game was over. I did it. I played in their game and I won.

When I was not jogging or playing ball, I spent much of my time in the neighborhood, reading on park benches. I was in Poe Park, reading, my basketball at my feet, when I heard someone say, "Stevie? Is that you?" I looked up to see a little old man in his seventies with the stub of a cigar sticking out of the corner of his mouth. He wore a sports shirt, white pants with suspenders, and he sup-ported himself with a cane. He was a much-aged version of Sam the bookmaker.

"It's Sam, Stevie."

"Sam!"

"I thought it was you," he said.

I jumped up and hugged him.

"Sam. Sam the Man!"

"I got old, Stevie."

"It's so good to see you, Sam!"

"Well, I'm alive. A lot of people are dead, but I'm alive. Moe and Rhoda Fisher—they're both dead."

"I didn't know that."

"Your father?"

"He's fine. He's in Florida."

"The candy store—it's not the same."

"I know."

"And next door they got a pizza place now," he said. "Two Puerto Rican brothers—they sell Italian pizza. You figure it."

"It's pretty good pizza."

"I'm not allowed to eat it. I'm one slice of pizza away from heaven."

"Sam!" I said, patting him on the back.

"Okay, gimme the leading scorers for Utah when they won the NIT?"

"Arnie Ferrin and Vern Gardner."

"Highest scorer, single game, college?"

"Bevo Francis. A hundred thirteen."

"That's my Stevie. You could have been a great bookie. I remember you when you were this high. You used to sit in the back of the candy store with comic books, reading with your lips."

"I'm probably reading with my lips again, Sam."

"So fill me in—advertising, I remember."

"It wasn't working out for me anymore."

"So?"

"So I travel in every day from Long Island and I hang around."

"It's summer. It's like you're on vacation, right?"

"People don't come to the Bronx, Sam. In the travel section of the *Sunday Times,* they don't advertise the Bronx. Maybe I've gone crazy."

"There's a fella walks along Jerome Avenue under the El and sings 'O Solo Mio' all day. *That's* crazy. Stevie, you remember Frankie Frisch with the Giant games?"

"He's batting two hundred, but he *l-o-v-e-s* to play ball."

"See? There's nothing wrong with you, Stevie."

We reminisced until dark about people from the neighborhood and sports events. We met every day from then on, to play cards and talk about the old days.

I discovered that on weekend mornings a different group of ballplayers showed up on the basketball court in St. James Park. These were "the older guys," which meant they were all at least twenty years younger than I. They were working men in their mid-twenties with a few college-age people as well. Their style of play was slower and closer to basketball as I had played it, people would sometimes pass off if they did not have a shot. I slipped into a game with them. I was beginning to get my touch back and in one streak my team stayed on the court for five games without losing. When the games ended, a stocky redheaded man in his late twenties named Jack Walsh said:

"You new around here?"

"I used to live around here."

"Well, maybe we'll see you tomorrow."

In schoolyard terms that was an outright invitation.

"Thanks. I'll see you."

I heard—or I hoped I heard someone say—"Good ballplayer," as they were leaving.

My life in the neighborhood became increasingly ritualized. I had my physical conditioning, my reading, my card games and conversations with Sam, my lunches at the candy store. Chris Anton was unraveling. He stood in the doorway watching people going into the coffee shop, the pizza place or the donut store, tallying lost revenue. "Another nail in my coffin," he would say. Chris had entered the business with his cousin, who then abandoned him to work in a luncheonette in Brooklyn, and Chris was left with long hours and small profits.

"They come in here for newspapers with their Big Mac containers in their hands. It's insulting."

Most of his business seemed to be with the sale of newspapers and magazines. The pizza store sold ices and ice cream cones, McDonald's served shakes, and they all competed for the local food business. I think I was the only person who ever ate in Chris' store. Everything was made fresh to order, he prepared nothing in advance because the poor man had no expectation that anyone would ever show up. So if I ordered a tuna sandwich, he would open a can of tuna. I ordered a hamburger and he went across the street and bought a hamburger patty from the butcher shop.

He told me about his family life, his daughter lived in Detroit, where she was married to an auto worker, his wife was a dressmaker in their apartment in Washington Heights. "Are you out of work, Steve?" he asked. "In a manner of speaking," I said to him. He patted me on the arm reassuringly.

Chris longed to visit the place where he had grown up, a village in Crete, and now he was in this place, where he had no heritage, and no sense of what this store he owned should be. He had little stock, he was relying on the sandwich trade to turn matters around for him, and there was a limit to how much I could eat.

"Chris, excuse me for meddling," I finally said to him. "But this store—it lacks detail."

"Detail?"

"Things. Items. Nickel-and-dime items, quarter items, dollar items. Things in cases and hanging from cards. Penlight batteries, rubber bands, ballpoint pens. Things that people don't know they need until they see them."

"You think?"

"It's too spare, Chris. And you should do something to get kids in here."

"They don't come. They buy pizza. They buy ices. They don't come to me."

"Get more comic books, Chris. And put them in the front. And bubble gum cards. And loose candy. I'm a big believer in loose candy for a candy store. It goes with the tradition. And it smells good."

"In the old days this worked?"

"In the old days this worked."

"Loose candy? Where do I get it?"

"There has to be a distributor."

I went to the public phone in the back and made a call.

"Mr. Robbins' office," my secretary answered.

"Hello, Miss Crawford."

"Mr. Robbins! Hello!"

"Miss Crawford, I want you to drop everything. Find out where you get the following items from a candy distributor: spearmint leaves, nonpareils, jujubes, licorice pipes, chocolate kisses, candy buttons, bubble gum cards, banana bats, and wax lips."

"Mr. Robbins?"

"Do you have that?"

"Yes."

"I'll call you in an hour."

I phoned and she gave me the names of two distributors in the city. Between them they had all of the items except the wax lips.

"When can we expect you back, Mr. Robbins?"

"No wax lips," I said, preoccupied. "It was a wonderful item. You could stick it over your lips and then eat it when it stopped being funny to you."

The next time I played ball with the older guys, Sam appeared at the fence to watch. When we were between games, he called out:

"It's big time today. You got yourself an All-City from Clinton."

"Really?" Jack Walsh said to me.

"Just honorable mention," I said.

"Still—"

"He scored thirty-four points once in a big game against Taft."

Bless Sam for remembering. It was 36 points, but I did not correct him. When we started to play again the change was subtle, but noticeable. I was getting the ball more often for shots. And I finally made the drifting-off-the-court push shot down the right side.

When we finished playing, Jack Walsh invited me to join them for a beer. We went to Shannon's Bar on Jerome Avenue, a long bar with pinball machines and a dart board to the side, and a color television set on a ledge over the bar. We talked basketball, I told them that when I first started to play nobody took jump shots, which a couple of them found hard to believe, and I recalled Red Holzman as a player, taking long, arching two-handed set shots. "Did you see the Original Celtics?" one of the younger ballplayers asked, missing my time by twenty-five years.

Sam tendered the invitation awkwardly, I sensed he was concerned that he would be rejected, or that I might have considered it inappropriate. He asked if I would join him and his wife for dinner at their home, and I said I would be pleased to come. On a Saturday night, I brought flowers for them, and entered Sam and Hinda Goodstein's apartment. Hinda was a lively little woman in her late sixties. The apartment, located near the reservoir, had summer slipcovers on the furniture and the aroma of mothballs in the air. They were like gnomes, they fluttered around, nervous about my being there. I was touched by how important a social occasion this was for them. Hinda had been a bookkeeper for an insurance office in the Bronx before she retired, and she had a memory for sports marginalia that equaled her husband's. She was the only sixty-nine-year-old woman I ever met who fondly remembered Native Dancer.

After a roast beef dinner, which we ate in the dining area, we sat in the living room for tea and cookies, the most expensive sold in the local bakery, purchased especially for their guest. I learned that they lived on Social Security and interest on the savings which they had accumulated. They went to neighborhood movies together, watched sports programs on television, played cards with friends. I admired what they had, a life together. They had had good racing luck. I wondered if I would ever reach old age with Beverly.

The time was after ten and I could see they were getting tired, but they did not want to end the evening. Sam brought out the family album, which contained pictures of their daughter Claire, who was a few years younger than I, scenes of Claire and her husband in New Rochelle with the grandchildren, and pictures of a younger Sam and Hinda in the neighborhood.

"What do you think of this?" Sam asked.

He showed me a picture taken in front of the candy store of Sam and a boy of seventeen.

"I'm in your book?"

"Sure. You were part of the candy store. Don't you remember?"

"Yes, Sam. I remember. I didn't know anyone else did."

I was becoming vain about my decreasing weight, so I avoided beer and whiskey at Shannon's Bar, ordering Tabs and eating sandwiches at the bar for dinner to build up my bar bill. The bartender, a burly man named O'Brien, was nonjudgmental, and I could sit at my leisure watching night ball games on television, chatting with some of the ballplayers whom I now knew. Jack Walsh was an insurance salesman, Jimmy Gomelli, at six feet three, the best ballplayer, was an auto mechanic, Jose Rudio and Mike Mazowski, two burly young men, worked for the Sanitation Department, Bobby Kelleher was a senior at St. John's University, Pete Hughes was a fireman. "What do you do, Steve?" Jack had asked me and I said, "Not much of anything right now." As an insurance man, he preferred more information. "What *was* your field?" he said, and I told him, "Advertising." That seemed to settle my account. I was scoring in the games and I had seen Bob Cousy play, which seemed to be more significant.

"Welcome to 'Wide World of Sports,'" Jack said to me as we were leaving the basketball court on a Saturday

morning. "How would you like to be our right fielder
today?"

"Your right fielder?"

"We've got a bar league. For softball."

"I don't know about that. I haven't played softball for
years."

"Come on, Clinton. We can't play without a right
fielder," and he put his arm around me and led toward
Jerome Avenue. We stopped at Shannon's and Jack said
to O'Brien, "Give the man a shirt," and the bartender
located a jersey with "Shannon's Bar" across the front
and the number 16 on the back.

"Jack, even when I played, this was not my best sport."

"Just don't throw the bat, and you'll be fine."

We walked toward Harris Field a few blocks away.
Our team consisted of the people I knew from the basketball court and some familiar faces from the bar. At the
ball field we linked up with a team from Leary's Tavern,
some wives and girlfriends came to watch, a few children
were there, beer and soda were set out in plastic ice containers. I did some stretching exercises, trotted around,
borrowed a glove and glided to the outfield, Joe D. In the
warm-up, a fly ball came to me, I had it all the way. "I got
it!" I called and settled under it. The ball went over my
head like a passing bird. I had no sense of the ball coming off the bat. Fly balls that seemed to be coming right
to me carried beyond me. I was lunging all over the place.
I must have looked like a Marcel Marceau parody of a
ballplayer. Everyone was given a few practice swings, I
failed to make contact several times, my best try was a
foul ball off third base. Eventually I caught a couple of

routine fly balls in practice, diving. Fortunately the ball game was incidental to the good-natured bench jockeying that went on between the two teams. I played a line drive into a triple, fielded a base hit and threw to the wrong base, and caught two pop flies, very unsteadily.

Leary's was ahead 10-7 in the eighth inning. I was the only man on our team not to reach base—0 for 4 on two taps to the pitcher, a popout to the catcher and a strikeout. In the bottom of the eighth with a man on third and one out, I managed to hit a slow grounder to the shortstop, was thrown out easily, but the run scored. My teammates cheered me with satiric "Way to hit, Steves" and Jack said to me, "An official RBI, slugger." We headed toward the bar afterward, talking about the game—Leary's had won 11-8. When we reached the bar I began to take my shirt off to return it.

"What's this?" Jack said. "You're on the team."

"You're kidding."

"You got an RBI and you didn't throw the bat."

"That's some record."

"Last week our right fielder drank too much beer and fell asleep out there."

"How many more games do you have?"

"Two."

"I'll try to practice."

"Don't do that," he said. "You'll screw up the system."

I drove back to Long Island wearing my Shannon's Bar shirt. I loved it. I wore it all the time.

In the last two games for Shannon's I actually got two base hits and made four putouts. Before we started the last game, Jimmy's wife, Cathy, a charming girl in her twenties, made us line up for a team photo. We posed early-baseball style with mock athletic gestures.

"Welcome to the major leagues, Steve," she said.

In the ball game, after I made a catch to end an inning, Jack came over to me.

"The season's ending too early for you, man. You're beginning to thrive."

"Like Yogi Berra when he played right field."

"You're doing fine."

"Well, I love my shirt. Where does this shirt go in the off season?"

"It's yours. Keep it."

In the top of the seventh, with Shannon's Bar leading the Emerald Saloon by the score of 5-4, the opposition's big hitter was struck out by Jack Walsh with two men on and one out to a chorus of "Yahoos" from our side. I shouted "Yahoo" also, loudly to the sky—not for the strikeout, but for my shirt, for standing in right field on a Saturday afternoon, for the simple fact of being alive and being there. "Yahoo!" I was still yelling after all the others had stopped.

Chapter 14

BY THE END of August I was working full-time in the candy store. My egg creams were made with the proper proportions of syrup, milk and seltzer, and my malteds were outstanding. Eat your heart out, McDonald's. The idea of a malted was to use cold, almost frozen, milk and enough malt so that it practically closes up your throat. McDonald's only made shakes, which are not malteds, as anyone who has tasted both can testify.

I realized that my advertising career was over. Tolchin could do as he pleased with the agency. Partners left agencies all the time, they retired, they died, they formed other agencies. The company would go on without me. There were young bloods in the firm, people wanting to be me—well, they could be me.

I would not be walking away from the agency with much money—we never ran that much ahead, but my family would be all right. I had put trust funds away for the girls' educations, we had the house, and its value had increased, and of course there was another business in the family. We were not bankrupt.

Chris Anton had offered me a job and I accepted. The appeal of the work to me was in how little it resembled what I had been doing. It seemed a perfect interim job until I could get myself settled—and I would be helping to save my candy store.

I called the office from the pay phone in the store.

"Ray, I'm pulling out of the agency."

"Taking what with you?"

"Nothing. It's all yours. We'll let the lawyers work it out."

"Steve, what's going on?"

"I've had it, Ray."

"Are you starting another shop?"

"No. I'm just through with cranking the stuff out."

"You're serious?"

"Yes, Ray."

"It figures. You've been really strange."

"So—there it is."

"You really want to resign?"

"Absolutely."

"Clean?"

"Right."

He thought about that for a moment, then he said:

"I don't want you stealing any of our accounts. You can't work for any of our accounts."

"Relax, Ray."

"And I'd want the right to keep the name—Robbins and Tolchin. There's continuity with a name. I own that too."

"Whatever you say."

"We'll get some papers drawn. When is this effective?"

"Immediately."

"Well, we can handle it."

"I don't hear you weeping."

"I'm not. So what are you doing, Steve? What's your plan?"

"I'm a soda jerk in a candy store in the Bronx."

"Very funny."

"I'm telling you the truth."

"Are you sober?"

"Totally."

"You're in the Bronx?"

"On Kingsbridge Road. If you're ever in the neighborhood, drop by. I'll make you a malted, so rich you wouldn't eat dinner."

Chris and I changed the front window, he had been using it as a counter for magazines, and we made it possible to serve drinks from the window to people standing on the sidewalk. We placed twine the length of the window and draped it with cardboard signs just as the Fishers had done in the old days, AUTHENTIC MALT MALTEDS, GENUINE EGG CREAMS, LIME RICKEYS, SODAS MADE TO ORDER, SUNDAES, FRAPPES—a distinction made for purists. We placed pegboard along the side of the store and covered the board with impulse items, increased the number of racks for magazines and comic books, filled a glass case with treasures—jacks, soap bubbles, rubber balls, magic tricks. We retained the griddle and the food counter, but we placed a new sandwich list on the wall, undercutting the coffee shop on price. And in the front of the counter we set out a display worthy of preservation in the Smithsonian, an assortment of loose candy in cardboard boxes, the good goods.

Chris opened the store early in the morning, I came in later in the morning and stayed until dinnertime. He went home to rest for a while when I was there, and then returned to close the store. Previously he had been exhausting himself trying to do everything on his own. I also came in for a few hours on Saturday, and this schedule still left me with time for athletics and for my card games with Sam—important commitments. I worked the front end of the counter in my white apron, the sodas, sundaes and malteds; Chris concentrated on the food items. I kept up a banter with our customers, I prepared everything with panache, and, frankly, I was having a very good time. I even created a sundae, the "Stevie's Special," ice cream topped with wheat germ and syrup.

"For this you went to college?" Sam asked me in the store.

"It's a lost art, Sam. So much comes packaged today."

"How much does he pay you?"

"Five dollars an hour."

"Well, you're between jobs, but you have a job in the meantime is how I see it," he said, working this out for himself.

Jack Walsh came in and I could see the look of surprise on his face to find me behind the counter. I was working on a big order for some teenagers at the time, two banana splits and a hot fudge sundae. I did it with flair, laying in each ingredient as though I were a chef.

The kids enjoyed me and *I* enjoyed me. I do not know if I suddenly lost status in Jack Walsh's view by doing this kind of work, but I was taking so much pleasure in what I did that he smiled, and he ordered a Stevie's Special. So if he had any reservations, I must have overcome them. He became a regular customer, as did several of the other ballplayers. They came in and we talked about sports and movies and events in the news—the kind of talk that went on in a neighborhood candy store. Along with whatever personal following I had, other customers were coming in, responding to the changes we had made, younger people who were now attracted to the place, and old timers who were getting a good candy store back again.

One day, a black chauffeured limousine slid past the store, and after several passes, the limousine stopped. A uniformed driver came out and opened the door for a man in a business suit, Ray Tolchin. He approached the store warily.

"Steve?"

"Hi, Ray. In the neighborhood?"

"You're really here!"

"I am."

"I don't believe it."

"Truth in advertising. I wouldn't lie to you."

He took a look at the surroundings.

"Do they know who you are?"

"They don't care."

A teenage boy came into the store.

"A black-and-white, Steve."

I made a chocolate soda with vanilla ice cream, capable now of directing the seltzer off the spoon.

"Jesus Christ!" my ex-partner said.

The chauffeur was lingering in the doorway.

"Is he your bodyguard?" I asked.

"I didn't know where I was going. I thought I could get mugged."

"I don't plan to mug you, Ray."

"Steve, what is this?"

"Just what you see. I quit the advertising business and I'm here."

"I don't know what I should do. Are you all right? Should I call a doctor?"

"I'm fine. *You* look a little pale."

He reached over the counter and patted me on the stomach.

"You lost weight. You're tan."

"Clean living. Light lunches with a little seltzer. No creative lunches, Ray."

"Look at you," he said, appraising me. "You're wearing an apron!"

"I don't think I should work in a suit."

"He's in a goddamn candy store!" He noticed the sign. "A *Stevie's Special?* You've got something named after you?"

"First an agency, and now a sundae. How many people in their lives can make such a claim?"

He sat down at the counter and rested his head in his hands.

"*He's* in a candy store and *I'm* dealing with Boujez."

"It all seems very remote to me."

"He wants product out by Christmas."

"Does he?"

"Actually, I hate that creep."

"Cheer up. How about a malted? On the house."

"I don't want a malted."

"Give yourself a treat."

"No! I'm not going to sit here and have you make me a malted."

"They walk blocks for my malteds."

"Steve, I don't want a malted!"

"Just taste it."

I made a malted and placed it on the counter. "You don't want to insult me, do you?"

"All right, goddammit. I'll taste your malted."

He sipped it.

"Well?"

"It's good."

"Good? Only good?"

"Excellent."

"Excellent?" I came out from behind the counter. "Is that the best malted you ever had?"

"Well, yes."

He drank a little more, unable to resist. We both began to laugh.

"You make a terrific malted, you maniac."

"Cold milk. That's the secret. Don't let that get out."

He stood up and went to look at the outside of the store.

"You sure dropped out." He looked at me closely. "You don't think I forced you out?"

"No, I don't."

"The lawyers are talking."

"That's good—"

"Steve, a candy store! Christ! I hope you don't object, but I'm not going to put this in the press release."

"I'm sure someone in the agency will find the right phrase to account for me."

We stood on the sidewalk, he in his suit, I in my apron.

"Are you really all right?" he asked.

"I wasn't. But I'm getting there."

I rose each morning in my house in the suburbs and made my way past the carefully tended lawns, one of which was ours. Beverly had made certain before she left for the summer that the gardener would still come by. Such was the attention to detail in a modern trial separation, the lawn was maintained. As I drove from suburbia to the Bronx there were mornings when I worried that I had managed to integrate a depression into a deeper, more serious state. But these fears would pass, usually when I arrived in the store and I saw the look of relief on Chris Anton's face, and when I watched people coming in, people who were now customers because of my suggestions for the place. My ideas there were working. I felt physically better than I had in years. I read books at night, I had energy. I could not have been crazy. This could not have been wrong for me, I reassured myself.

The summer was ending and the girls wrote to ask if I would meet their bus at the Port Authority Terminal on the Saturday they were due to arrive. I was waiting for them in my Shannon's Bar shirt, which had become my number one dress shirt. In keeping with their respective styles, Amy and I hugged each other, Sarah and I exchanged discreet kisses.

"What are you *wearing?*" Sarah asked.

"It's very fashionable," I said, "Jock chic."

For a moment she was uncertain and I spared her the awkwardness.

"I'm on a team."

"You?" she said.

I took their bags and we walked to the car.

"How was the summer?" I asked.

"Good," Amy said, Sarah offered an "Okay."

"But how was yours, Daddy?" Amy asked. "You look fantastic."

I had lost fifteen pounds, and was still working on it.

"When Mommy gets back I'll tell you all about it."

On the ride home I received their report on counselor life in the Berkshires, but I lost benefit of their company minutes after we arrived at the house, as they disappeared to make phone calls to friends. I had anticipated this and had booked them into dinner at a restaurant so I could keep them with me a while longer. I put on a sports jacket and a different shirt for the occasion.

"I'm glad you changed," Sarah said as we got into the car.

"Number 16 is one of the great shirts," I answered.

"You're not really on a team, are you? It must be some advertising thing."

They had been told, when they were younger, that I had been a ballplayer in school. Obviously they had forgotten. It was not within their frame of reference. I stopped the car.along the way. Two boys were playing basketball at a backboard on a garage.

"I want to show you something," I said to my daughters.

I walked over to the boys and asked if I could borrow their ball for a minute.

"Daddy, what are you doing?" Amy said.

"Before dinner you get the floor show."

I escorted the girls out of the car to the side of the driveway, where they stood, impatient with me. I took the basketball and fast-dribbled it close to the ground, shifting left hand to right like a bongo player. I dribbled up to the basket, made a right-handed layup, then a left-handed layup, then a right-hander backhand from the left side, and a left-hander backhand from the right side, took a few one-handers, close in range, and made a couple, dribbled back to the girls, then headed down the center and dropped in a floating layup, underhand. I faked a pass to one of the boys, whipped the ball around my back, rolled it off my arm, flicking it into the air with my fingertips, back into the boy's hands.

The girls seemed astonished—that I had done all this—that I *could* do it.

"That's amazing, Daddy," Amy said. Even Sarah said, "Great."

"You better believe it."

As they stared at me, I walked back to the car—very jauntily.

Chapter 15

BEVERLY CALLED THE house to say she would be coming back after Labor Day. "How did the summer go?" I asked. "It was inconclusive," she replied. And then the conversation became cluttered with details, what time of day she would be back, whether the girls would be going out there for Labor Day weekend, when Sarah was leaving for Vassar, when the cleaning woman had last been in, whether the gardener had shown up. "This is so logistical," I said, "it's like we're in the army." "That's been one of the problems," she answered. In two minutes it seemed that we were right back where we were before—and she wasn't even home yet, and she didn't even *know* yet.

The girls decided to visit Beverly in Montauk, I had an invitation to a party at Jack Walsh's apartment for Saturday night. I worked for a few hours that day, then met Sam in Poe Park for our card game. He had been looking better. I think it was good for Sam to be with someone who remembered him from his glory days.

"How's the Malted King?" he asked, teasing me.

"We were busy today."

"So when are you going to get a real job?" he asked, as we began to play cards.

"I have a job, Sam."

"Something in advertising—*that* would be a job. This is a bad time in advertising?"

"It is for me."

"Stevie, don't be insulted, but I have a friend, who has a son, who works in advertising. An account executive?"

"Yes, that's a job."

"This place, they do the ads for a lot of big stores. I could talk to my friend and he could talk to his son."

"That's kind of you, Sam, but I'm not *in* advertising anymore. Thank you."

We played cards and talked about the coming football season, then Sam became pensive.

"You know, I don't have too many seasons left, Stevie."

"Don't say that. You've been getting younger since I've been coming around."

"My daughter wants me and Hinda to go down to Florida for the winter."

"Well, you could move the card season to a warmer bench."

"This is my home. Here I got the Knicks. I got the Rangers. I got the Jets. What do they have there? The Miami Dolphins? I don't root for any team that's the name of a fish."

We left the park and strolled until we reached Sam's house.

"Listen, you were going to bring me a picture of your family."

I had promised Sam that I would, and I removed a snapshot from my wallet, a picture taken at the anniversary party—Beverly, Sarah, Amy and I standing in front of a cake.

"Stevie, this is some beautiful family."

"Yes," I said, looking at the picture. "They're only gorgeous."

It began to rain after I left Sam and I went into the candy store and sat in the rear, reading a book. Chris was busy in the front with his figures. He was compulsive about bookkeeping, and now that the store had more traffic, he occupied himself projecting costs and profits.

"Steve, all the drinks of the summer—what happens in the cold weather?"

"There has to be a dropoff. You *do* have hot chocolates."

"Hot chocolates."

But Chris needed something else to compete with the other businesses in the area. I recalled that The Fishers had once used a "frozen malted" machine, which dispensed what was actually ice milk. Purist that I was, a machine seemed acceptable, it was in the original charter.

"Frozen yogurt," I said to Chris. "It's very big these days. Nobody around here is selling it—and you could put a machine in and have cones and cups, and different kinds of toppings."

"Frozen yogurt! Steve, you're a genius!"

The word certainly took on different meanings in different settings.

I ate dinner at Shannon's Bar, bought a bottle of wine at a liquor store to bring to Jack Walsh's party, and went to his apartment in a gray brick building on the Grand Concourse. Jack's wife, Terry, a tall, pretty redhead in her twenties, far along in her pregnancy, met me at the door.

"Steve. I'm glad you could come."

Jack came forward, gave me a warm greeting and led me to a bar in the living room. Several guests had already arrived—Jimmy and his wife, Cathy, and a few of the other ballplayers with their dates and wives. I exchanged greetings with them, and Jack introduced me to a young woman named Nancy Reilly. She was a slim brunette wearing a sweater and dungarees, pretty, with short hair and a pug nose. Jack stepped away to meet someone at the door, and we were standing at the bar together.

"So you're Steve."

"Have you ever heard of me?"

"No, I just thought I'd say that."

"Nancy, I'm going to ask you something that's going to make me feel ancient. How old are you?"

"How old do you think I am?"

"Please don't embarrass us both."

"I'm twenty-four."

"Twenty-four. I see. Well, if you're twenty-four, then I must be forty-five."

"You look younger."

"Thank you, I think."

I turned to Jack and Terry who were standing nearby.

"When is the baby due?"

"Any time next month."

I had revealed very little to these people about my personal life. "I have children," I said, and I removed the snapshot from my wallet.

"This is my wife, Beverly—she has an art school for kids. My daughter, Sarah. She's eighteen. She'll be a freshman at Vassar. My daughter, Amy. She's keeping the planet in ecological balance."

"It's a great looking family, Steve," Terry said.

"I didn't even know you were married," Jack remarked. "You could have brought your wife."

"I don't know if she would have come. We're sort of non-marrieds at the moment."

"What does non-married mean?" Nancy asked.

"That we've been separated for the summer, but we're not officially separated—whatever *that* means."

As the party progressed, I sat on the couch, other people were seated on chairs in a semicircle and we talked about children and schools and crime in the neighborhood. Street crime was not at the level of other neighborhoods in the Bronx, but Terry said there were enough incidents for her to be concerned. Jack felt she was building a case for moving to the suburbs. Terry suggested he did not want to move because he would miss his ballplaying. The conversation drifted to inflation, to movies—I had a standing as a movie expert, "Say, Steve, did you see . . . ?" It was a rambling discussion. Important to me was that I was part of this group, no special effort was being made to include me—I was included.

Cold cuts were served, in a back bedroom people were dancing to disco music. The evening became boozy, the disco room was heavy with marijuana smoke. Someone put slower music on the stereo, a few of the younger couples were necking in the corners of the apartment, a scene I had not witnessed in decades.

Nancy Reilly sat down next to me on the couch.

"Jack tells me you used to be in advertising."

"Yes."

"And now you work in a candy store?"

"I do."

"What's that all about?"

"I've changed careers."

"Jack?" she called out. "Is this guy okay?"

"Steve? Sure he is."

"He says he's in the candy store because he changed careers?"

"Guys are doing more of that. We had a whole meeting on it. That's why we're pushing major medical."

"Not here, Jack," I said.

"What did you do in advertising?" she said.

"A lot of things. My specialty, if you can call it that, was copy—ideas, words."

"And now you're in a candy store. You must be a very weird guy, or very interesting. Which is it—interesting?"

"God, I hope so."

We sat there a few moments, watching the party, then Nancy asked me:

"Would you like to dance?"

"Sure. The Return of the Box Step."

We went into the next room to dance. As we were dancing, Nancy told me that she hoped to leave the Bronx and move to an apartment downtown. She was a teller at a bank on Fordham Road, she and a girlfriend, her prospective roommate, were planning their escape. She pressed her body close to mine and placed her cheek against my face. I closed my eyes, and remembered all this from another time. "When do their parents come home?" I said.

She drew nearer to me. I did not know how far to pursue the dance. I started thinking of Sam and Hinda and how I wanted Beverly and me to be that close. The way to get there was not with twenty-four-year-old Nancy Reilly, a pretty girl who pressed herself against me very tightly when we danced.

"Nancy, I'm sorry."

"For what?"

"I have to go."

I thanked Jack and Terry, said goodbye to the others and drove back to Long Island, wondering what Beverly would think of the essay I was going to hand in on My Summer Vacation.

Chapter **16**

ON SUNDAY, TWO days before Beverly's return, I was sitting alone in the house and I decided that what I needed was a dog. I had never owned a dog. We were never a dog family. Sarah had allergies. Nobody wanted the bother. I felt that what was called for me next was a dog, a dog who could wear two hats, as it were, and adjust to both suburban and neighborhood life. Jerry Rosen had a dog and I did not. Other people had dogs. If I were doing a revise of my life, then this was something I had never done before. I would own a dog. Beverly would return and I would get it all in—in one shot. She would be confronted by the entire new me.

I had dog standards. No pedigrees. It would have to be an authentic Bronx dog, a mutt. Since my need was for an immediate dog, I had limited resources, the ASPCA was closed for the Labor Day weekend. So I set out for the Bronx in the hope of making a canine score with my street contacts.

In a corner of St. James Park there usually congregated a tough-looking group of men in their twenties and thirties with radios and cassette players producing disco music loud enough to contact life on other planets. As a park regular and a dispenser of refreshments in the neighborhood, I had a passing "Whatdayasay?" relationship with several of them, and a few played basketball now and again in our games. At times I had been offered a drink out of a brown paper bag or a drag of marijuana as they milled around. I declined these offers, but I had the feeling that if I ever wanted to buy something, anything, these were the people to see. They were there when I arrived, one of the ballplayers I knew was leaning against a bench, drinking beer. He was an Hispanic in his early twenties named Joe, a small, wiry man who went through all kinds of weather shirtless, his shirt usually tied around his neck. "Whatdayasay?" I said, and "Whatdayasay?" he said.

"I'm looking to buy a dog," I told him, and I was immediately concerned that "dog" might be some street code word for something else.

"A dog, huh?" He took a swig of his beer. "Guy want to buy a dog," he said to his drinking companions. This was not the most important news they ever received. They barely looked up.

"I like to walk a dog," I said, to make sure we were talking about the same item.

He was deep in thought. He took another swig of beer, then he nodded as though it all came into focus.

"How big?"

It was a question I had not considered, and I held out my hand and lowered it, trying to find a size.

"Guy I heard of—he can get you hot dogs," he said.

"Hot dogs?"

"Guy I heard of—he steal dogs, fancy dogs, and he sells 'em."

"Oh, hot dogs," I said. At least we were talking about dogs.

"You want a fancy dog?" he asked.

"I want a not-hot dog."

"A legal dog?" Joe said.

"Right."

"Then maybe you should try Gomez," Joe said to me. "He has dogs."

"Legal?"

"Yeah, Gomez. Marion Avenue. Twenty-six forty-two. He the super. Try him."

"Thanks a lot, Joe."

"Sure. Get a dog who don't make," he said, needling me. "They more money, but they the best kind."

Gomez lived on the other side of the Grand Concourse in the next neighborhood. The building was an old walk-up. I asked an elderly woman sitting on the steps of the building if she knew where the super was, and she pointed to the side entrance. I walked through a dark alleyway to the back, cautiously. "Mr. Gomez?" I called out and suddenly there was a loud howling of dogs. Gomez appeared, a muscular man in his forties, wearing overalls and smoking a pipe.

"Joe sent me," I said. "I want to buy a dog."

"I have dogs."

I followed him to the door of a carriage room, he opened it and a yelping and barking came from what must have been a dozen dogs of every size, and they all came toward me at once. I leaped outside and slammed the door.

"How can you buy a dog," he said, coming out to talk to me, "if you afraid of a dog?"

"I'm not afraid of *a* dog. I'm not sure about twelve dogs."

"Wait," he said. "I tie 'em up," and he went back inside. In a few minutes he returned and led me inside. The dogs were tied by ropes and leashes to radiators and plumbing pipes. The room was bare with a naked light bulb hanging from the ceiling, dogs everywhere.

"All good dogs," he said. "All healthy."

"They have strong voices."

I tried to get close in order to make the rounds of the personnel, but they started barking again.

"Maybe I should settle for a cat."

"You want a cat. I have cats."

"No, I'll try to work this out."

I approached one dog, a large mutt, and tried to pet him and he wagged his tail. More confident now, I worked my way around the room, patting heads. They were not killers, although they could have fooled me.

"You want more than one, I give good price."

Some enchanted evening, you may see a stranger. I saw him, my dog, a fox terrier, some kind of terrier. A more accurate description would be to call him a brown dog. He was smallish with a cute face, a tough little body, a bushy tail. If ever there was a prototypical mutt—this was it.

"You like him?"

I reached down and petted the dog and he got very

excited and started moving his entire body while wagging his tail.

"This smart dog. Watch. Sientate! Dame la pata!"

The dog followed his commands, sat, gave him a paw.

"Does he speak English?"

"You have to teach him."

Gomez untied the dog and I walked outside with them.

"Does he have a name?"

"Ramon. He Puerto Rican dog."

"How much, Mr. Gomez?"

"Thirty-seven fifty."

"This is not a champion here."

"Healthy dog. He has license. I give you the leash."

"It's a little high."

"Okay, twenty-nine fifty."

They had very strange prices at the Gomez Kennels.

"And I throw in a cat."

"I don't need a cat just now."

I looked at the dog.

"For that kind of money," I said, "he should be a dog who doesn't make."

"A dog who don't make!" Gomez thought this was very funny. I was cross-pollinating park humor.

"It's really Joe's joke," I said.

"For you, twenty-two fifty."

"You've got a deal."

"You got a dog."

As I walked along the street, I kept bursting into laughter checking my appearance in the reflection of store windows. I was walking my dog. I drove home, stopping for dog food on the way. I was going to need a book on dogs, I presumed there was a Dr. Spock equiva-lent on the subject. I put an old blanket on the floor of the guest room, where he slept that night. The next day I gave him a bath, a "Pete Smith Specialty" right there—"Will the floor be flooded with *some* of the water from the tub? *Most* of the water from the tub? You're wrong. He got *all* of the water from the tub onto the floor." After the bath, the dog looked fluffy and clean, although still his muddy brown. "Nervous?" I said to the dog as we waited for Beverly. I had discovered the secret about dog owners—they talked to their dogs. "You could be my therapist," I said to the dog. "Dr. Ramon, the eminent caninist." He appraised me. "If it doesn't work, we can always try group therapy. And get several dogs."

The station wagon pulled into the driveway and I took the dog by the collar and we stood in the doorway. Bev-erly got out of the car, followed by the girls. She was wearing a denim work shirt and dungarees, deeply tanned, her blond hair bleached lighter by the sun. She was beautiful.

"Hi, old friend," I said. I walked to her and put my arms around her. She patted my arm neutrally and gave me a kiss on the cheek.

"You look extraordinary, Steve. Being away from me must agree with you."

"It doesn't."

"What is *that?*"

"My dog."

"You got yourself a dog?" Beverly said.

Amy leaned down to pet him.

"What's his name, Daddy?"

"Ramon. He's a bilingual dog."

"He's very homely," Sarah said.

"He's pure mutt. I bought him from a super. A super's dog. You can't get any more authentic than that."

"You mean you actually went out and bought this creature?" Beverly said.

"It was a cash deal. With an option on an undisclosed cat to be named at a later date."

"Really, now."

"Come on in. I have some things to tell you."

We all sat down in the living room. I had their attention. The dog seemed to have served as a visual aid.

"This summer I went through a very bad time. A personal crisis, you might call it."

"Steve?"

"I'm okay now. But at the time, nothing seemed right to me. Not our marriage, Bev—as we all knew. Not my work. Nothing."

"Oh, Steve—"

"It was like I was lost. Then I remembered my old neighborhood. And I went back there. And I got myself together."

"Where?" Sarah said.

"In the Bronx."

"The Bronx?"

"First, I just—hung around. Then I began to get into shape. Then I went so far as to get a job there. I couldn't have two jobs, so I resigned from the agency."

"What?" Beverly said.

"Tolchin was not all that unhappy, I must say."

"You resigned?" Sarah said.

"When I was a kid I had this image—I was going to be an advertising man. I was going to be sophisticated and well-dressed and very un-Bronx. And when I got there, it was just a meaningless game of being clever."

Beverly was shaking her head, the girls were staring at me.

"You might as well get it all. I'm working in a candy store."

"Daddy!" Amy said. "That's not funny."

"Yes, Daddy, it's a very bad joke," Sarah said.

Beverly knew that I was not joking.

"A candy store, Steve?"

"What are you saying, Daddy? I'm supposed to go to college!"

"You can still go to college. You can go to as many colleges as you want. I put the money away for you."

"I don't believe it," Amy said. "It's so embarrassing."

"The people there are very decent. They've treated me kindly. I'm not embarrassed to be with them."

"Daddy, how can you be so smart and do something so incredibly dumb?" Sarah said.

"None of this is very easy to tell you about. What I'd like is for you to come there and see what I'm involved in—"

"No, thank you," Sarah said.

"I'm not going to any Bronx," Amy added.

"Steve!"

"I made a change in my life. People change, Bev. *You* did."

"But to do this—"

She sat, shaking her head, frowning. They were all

avoiding my eyes. I insisted that they should at least give me the courtesy of going through the neighborhood with me to see why the place was so important to me. Beverly consented to come, the girls declined. The best I extracted from them was that they would take care of the dog while I was out of the house. Beverly went off to unpack, no one was interested in dinner. I seemed to have ruined their appetites.

Later in the evening I walked the dog, and when I returned, Beverly was already in bed, her eyes closed.

"Bevvy—"

"I was almost sleeping."

I tried to put my arms around her, she edged away. I kissed her on the neck, she was unresponsive.

"If ever I was not in the mood," she said.

I ran my fingers over her body.

"No, Steve—"

I became fevered, kissing her, touching her. Two months away from her. She began to respond, slowly, it was a conflicted emotion, she would alternately shake her head, no, then embrace me, but she became moist and I entered her, and as I did I was clenching my teeth, I was competing with whoever else she had known— before the summer, during the summer, competing with her recollections of me. I would show her I was feeling strong, that I was physically able, if nothing else. She summoned a physicality of her own that I could not recall, and when we had come, we lay still, impatient to begin again. I lasted longer the next time, until we finally stopped, drained, wet from perspiration and each other. She spoke the only words that had passed between us from the time I had begun to kiss her.

"Goddamn you!" she said.

I called Chris to tell him I would not be at work, we had been breaking in a college student, a young woman, as a part-time worker, and she would fill in for me. Beverly went to her office for a few hours and in the afternoon we were ready to leave. She was wearing gray slacks, a blouse and a jacket, collar up in the fashion, I was in a sport shirt, light sweater, dungarees and sneakers— my street clothes. We drove into the city talking about the girls and some of Beverly's plans for the year at the Institute. When we reached the neighborhood I had an urge to get out and pick up litter so that it would all look cleaner to her.

"I remember some of this from when your mother died," she said.

"I was surprised anything was still here."

I drove past the college to Harris Field and then around the reservoir, joggers were out, the area was green with summer.

"It's not a bad place," I said, selling.

I parked on Jerome Avenue and led Beverly into St. James Park. A teenager came running in our direction, Beverly stopped walking and froze in fear. Without breaking stride, the teenager slapped skin with me, said, "Stevie, baby," and kept running. He was one of the regulars in the candy store.

"You're known, I see. Thank God."

"It's my neighborhood."

I led her toward the basketball courts, the teenagers were there in one of their wild, scrambling games.

"I'm going to play."

Their game ended, we shot baskets for a few minutes, then I joined in the next game. I dominated the game.

"Incredible," she said, when I walked off the court.

"The point is, I've gotten myself in shape." I smiled and added, "And I think I played very well."

We went to Poe Park, a block away.

"This is a cultural stop," I said. "Edgar Allan Poe wrote there."

"When he wasn't playing basketball."

"They used to have dances here. Maybe he did the fox-trot."

I looked for Sam, I expected him to be there, and I saw him sitting at his favorite bench, reading a newspaper.

"I want you to meet a friend—" and I guided Beverly over to him.

"Sam—"

"Stevie!"

"Sam Goodstein, Beverly Robbins. This is my wife, Sam."

He jumped to his feet and shook Beverly's hand.

"I'm so happy to meet you," he said.

Out of nervousness, Sam was trying to make clothing adjustments to neaten his appearance.

"Nice to meet you, Mr. Goodstein."

"Call me Sam. I'm Sam. You know how long I know this fella?"

"How long?"

"Long," he said, looking at me. "Long."

"Sam and I meet, we play cards, we talk about sports."

"He has a good mind, your husband."

"Yes, he does."

"It's hard to stump him. Best career batting average—Williams, Musial or DiMaggio?" Sam said, wanting to show off his protege.

"Williams. Three forty-four."

"See?" Sam said, pleased.

"Bet you didn't know I knew that."

"I don't even know what you're talking about."

"So beautiful a girl, Stevie. You're the most beautiful girl in the Bronx today."

"Thank you, Sam," she said.

"I'm showing Beverly the neighborhood. You're a stop on the cultural tour."

"Am I? You know what I used to do for a living?" he asked Beverly.

"No."

"I was a bookmaker, a bookie. But trustworthy."

"I'm sure."

"There's not many of us around anymore. Poe gets a cottage. Maybe for me they'll erect a phone booth."

"See you, Sam," I said.

"I'm glad to have met you," he said to Beverly. "Goodbye, Sam."

I brought Beverly to Shannon's Bar, where we ordered Tabs at the end of the bar. The place was beginning to get busy with people stopping for beers on the way home from work. None of the ballplayers were there, a couple of people I knew from the bar made detours to say hello so they could get a close look at Beverly. I pointed out a photo of the Shannon's Bar softball team, taped to the bar mirror. "Recognize anyone?"

She examined the photo.

"You're on their team?"

"Isn't that something?"

"Yes. It is." She looked into my eyes, studying me. "Let's see this famous candy store."

Chris was at the rear when we arrived, working on his receipts.

"Chris, I'd like you to meet my wife. Chris Anton. Beverly Robbins."

"Your wife?" He came forward, staring at Beverly baldly, looking at her clothes. "I didn't know Steve had such a wife."

"He's very tricky," Beverly said.

"This man—you have no idea how he saved me. I was going to be devoured by the Big Mac. He fixed this up, the candies, the specialties. Nobody knows the candy-store business like your husband."

"Is that so?"

She looked at the signs hanging in the window.

"You wrote the copy?" she said to me.

"The copy and the concept," I answered dryly.

"Would you like something, please, Mrs.?"

"Sure, let me make you a malted or an egg cream," I said.

"An egg cream?"

"My California angel, it's not made with an egg."

I stepped behind the counter.

"Chocolate syrup, milk, seltzer. My secret is—I put the milk in first, then the seltzer—" I did my off-the-spoon routine. "Then the syrup." I stirred it up, producing a chocolate drink with a white foam head.

"Wonderful," she said, tasting it.

"Technically you're supposed to drink it straight down, but we'll give you an amnesty."

"I appreciate that."

Two teenagers came in while I was standing there and ordered vanilla egg creams, which I prepared as Beverly watched, with an amused expression on her face.

As we were walking back to the car, she said:

"I'll grant you one thing—it's sort of brave of you, in a way. People drop out of careers, but not to do *this.*"

"I'm happy here, Bev."

"So I see. But aren't you going to get bored making egg creams?"

"I also read a lot. I didn't think you wanted to observe me reading."

"You were right."

She was quiet, thoughtful on the drive back to Long Island, and when we stopped for dinner in a restaurant she stayed in this mood. At home, Beverly went to the room she used as an office, saying she had paper work to do, and I read in the bedroom. I went to sleep after eleven, Beverly had not yet come to bed. I awoke at two in the morning, and saw that she was not lying next to me. I went into the living room and found her there. She was on the couch, pensive, sitting in the dark. I sat down next to her.

"I think I understand what you've been doing," she said.

"Do you, Bev?"

"Yes. If you were that upset I can see where you might do something like you did."

"I just couldn't go on in advertising, Bev. I came to the end."

"I see that, I guess. But you didn't choose the classiest job I ever heard of. Our marriage has not been wonderful. This job was not going to save our marriage."

"I thought I'd start by saving myself."

"And I've been worrying about *myself,*" she said. "I'm afraid I didn't think about you very much this summer, Steve."

"You didn't?"

"I was happy to be away. I had time of my own. I could think about what I wanted to do next."

"Which is?"

"Steve, I want to be the best I can—just like you wanted to be. Is that wrong?"

"No."

"Well, I was thinking I could do more, I could set up a franchise, sell the program to other cities."

"I suppose you could—"

"And I could get into adult education, build up a night program—"

"Yes, I'm sure you'd be able to—"

"Except we hardly see each other now. And am I willing to give up all that, just for our marriage? And I don't think I am."

"That's blunt enough."

"And now I come back and see where you are—God! You're trying to simplify things for yourself, and I haven't gotten *enough* for myself."

We sat in the dark and then I said what could not be denied any longer.

"We're just in different places, Bev. It can't work."

I put my arm around her, she moved close to me and we stayed like that a long time, trying to comfort each other. The sadness in the room was overwhelming.

I don't know what else we might have done. I had pursued my ambitions and she had pursued hers, and we had lost each other along the way. We told the children, but they already knew. I tried to keep busy in the days that followed. It was never out of my mind for very long. If I was thinking of something else, it was as though a voice would call out to me, taunting, "Hey, Steve, did you forget? You and Bevvy are finished." I don't know. She was so pretty I could cry.

Soon after I came full circle in this. I moved into an apartment in my old neighborhood. I moved there because I was getting a divorce and would no longer be living in the house, and because I did not want to be in the suburbs with its shopping malls, and because I did not give a damn anymore about being an executive and being in advertising. I was trading it in, as with baseball cards, "I'll give you a Mel Ott for a Bob Feller. . . ." I was trading in my dreams of the fifties for a new beginning.

Chapter **17**

" '**ANTIMACASSAR.' THAT'S A** wild word, isn't it, Sam? Do you know what it comes from?"

"From somebody's aunt?"

"Anti—against. Macassar—which used to be a hair oil people used on their heads. Anti-macassar."

"I never saw a fella so interested in *tchotchkas*."

Sam helped me get an apartment on a sublease in a red brick building near the reservoir. The previous occupants, an elderly couple, friends of Sam's, left behind an old green wing chair. Hanging from beneath the seat was a tag originally meant for the retailer with the admonition "Do Not Remove This Tag Under Penalty of Law," which the couple had dutifully obeyed for thirty years. I decided not to remove the tag either, the tag had given me an idea. I fixed up the apartment with clean, modern pieces, but inspired by that chair with the tag I turned a section of the living room into a nostalgia corner. I went to junk shops, flea markets, antiques stores in Manhattan, looking for great old evocative pieces from the forties, when I was growing up in the neighborhood. I found the antimacassars for the chair, and an art deco snake lamp whose base culminated in a nymph, a serving tray painted with the trylon and perisphere from the World's Fair, and a majestic Philco console pushbutton radio with the original station call letters, WEAF, WJRZ, WOV. I had a good time searching for these old pieces, which were marvelous.

I wrote a letter to my father, telling him about Beverly and about the agency, composing it carefully, wanting to get it right. I realized that the traffic in Florida was in children's success stories and I had given my father difficult material to work with. He sent me a kind note in reply:

"Dear Steve. I'm very sorry to hear about you and Beverly. Nothing I can say will make it better, but I want you to know that all around me I hear from people who stayed in marriages that were not good and ended up being bitter. So I think this is for the best, even if it is more painful right now. As for your work, I can only tell you I worked for years in a job I didn't really like. I'm proud of you for being stronger than I ever was. Frankly, I think you can do better than a candy store, but that's up to you. In the meantime, there's a guest room here if you ever feel like being a loafer for a while. I'm buying. Love, Dad."

I changed seasons with the guys in the neighborhood, we were playing touch football now on the weekends. I was an acceptable pass receiver and played with my faithful hound, Ramon, tied to a fence. His English was improving.

Jack Walsh called to say that Terry Walsh had given birth to a girl and I visited with them in the hospital to wish them well. I became a regular at Shannon's for Monday night football, met with Sam and Hinda for occasional dinners and sports events on television, and went downtown to Manhattan for museums and movies.

At the candy store, Chris was concerned, as always, with his receipts.

"We have to do more business," he said, thumbing through the books. "What about omelets?" he asked. "I can make good omelets. I've only been making eggs."

He looked at me, concerned, waiting for my approval.

"I have no objection to omelets," I said.

Pleased, he put his hand on my shoulder.

"Someday, Steve, we'll have our dream."

I was interested to know just what Chris thought this shared dream would be.

"And what's that, Chris?"

"People standing behind people sitting," he said with emotion.

After a Sunday morning touch football game at Harris Field I walked back toward Kingsbridge Road with Jack Walsh. We talked about his baby and what it meant to both of us to be a father for the first time. Then I remembered I needed some items for the house and I said instinctively, "Would you walk me to the store?" Jack went with me to the grocery and when we came out we strolled on toward my house.

"Steve, how you doing there—behind the counter?"

"I'm doing all right."

"Terry and I were talking about you. We were wondering if you're a little overqualified for the job."

"Not to Chris. He thinks I'm perfect."

"But you *could* be doing something else."

"I could. I don't want to right now."

"Well, whatever you do, you'll do good at it," he said, wanting to encourage me.

"Thank you for that, Jack."

It had been a long time since a buddy had walked me anywhere.

I had been speaking to Sarah and Amy regularly by phone and was able to receive information about their activities, they were less than enthusiastic in hearing about mine. My daughters were obviously embarrassed by having their father in the Bronx. It was as though they had discovered I was an alcoholic and were tentative about dealing with my "condition." So we met on neutral ground, Amy and I had lunches and dinners in Manhattan, and I traveled up to Poughkeepsie to spend time with Sarah. The talk was mostly about them, which I accepted as the terms of the meetings, I was more concerned with being able to see them.

Amy ate no meat for ideological reasons, and now she was boycotting fish. At a restaurant, the waitress announced the day's special was stuffed sole, and Amy said to her, "Commercial fishermen are the looters of the sea!" She ordered a vegetable plate and in deference to Amy I ordered a salad. I was not the subject of the

conversation, we talked this day about the survival of
the porpoise and the snail darter. I was, frankly, becoming bored with fish talk, and mentioned that my new
friends, the Walshes, had a baby girl, which reminded
me of the times when both Amy and Sarah were little.
Suddenly, Amy said:

"Daddy, why did you do such a thing?"

"That sounds like 'Say it ain't so, Joe.' I don't think
I've done anything bad. If you mean divorcing, it's not
what I would have wanted. If you mean my job, it's not a
criminal activity."

"What am I supposed to tell people?"

"That your father is a very interesting man. That after
twenty years, the work he was doing didn't mean anything to him and instead of committing suicide he got
himself reborn. That ought to get their attention."

"Oh, Daddy, I love you. I hope you're okay."

"I'm okay."

"Are you lonely?"

"Yes. Some." And I reached out to touch her face. "But
not right now, darling."

I think the girls must have been talking about me
because when I next visited Sarah she seemed more
interested than before in how I was getting along. At one
point she said:

"It must be hard there—in the Bronx. I mean, intellectually. What's there?"

"Actually, I read more now that I'm there than I have in
years. And I go downtown. I go to galleries and museums."

"Well, Amy and I don't have a system yet for telling
people about you."

"Think of me this way. I'm marching to a different drummer. He just happens to be with the Glenn Miller band."

She smiled and said:

"Why didn't you just run off to some commune? I could have explained you better."

"You don't have to explain me at all, darling," I said, kissing her on the forehead. "Just stay in my life."

I called Nancy Reilly, and after expressing her annoyance with my abrupt departure that night at the Walsh's party, she agreed to an evening with me. She asked if I would meet her on a street corner and I suspected she did not want her parents to see me because I would have seemed too old for her. I asked about this and she said, "No. I just don't want them to know my business."

Nancy was a person preoccupied with getting out of her present situation and being on her own.

"If I move in with a roommate, we can go to six hundred a month rent, but if I do it alone, I can only go to maybe three-fifty, and for that, you get a place where you have to live in one room. Or else it's Brooklyn or Queens and who needs that? I'm already in the *Bronx*."

She was so high-keyed that if she smoked she would have been a chain smoker. As it was, she kept popping candy mints in her mouth. I wanted to kiss her just for the mintiness of it, and also to calm her down for a moment. She converted everything back to her main interest. Over dinner, out of curiosity, she asked if she might have seen any of the ads I had written when I was in advertising. I mentioned a few of the campaigns I had worked on and she was genuinely surprised, but then asked me if many women worked in the office. When I said there were quite a few, she wanted to know if they all had their own apartments.

We had gone to Chinatown for dinner and, at my suggestion, we went to a revival of a Preston Sturges comedy at the Bleeker Street Cinema. When I had first seen it, Nancy was not even born yet. The audience was filled with young people I presumed were film buffs. It was between myself and one member of a male couple as to who was the oldest person in the theater. Nancy was also thinking of the demographics.

"See all these people? I'm the only one here who still lives at home with her parents in the Bronx."

She laughed at her own humor, but only slightly.

"There are worse places to be," I told her.

"*You* can say that. You don't live at home with *your* parents. And you don't live at home with *my* parents."

In the car on our way uptown, we stopped at a light near an apartment building that was under construction and Nancy began to estimate what the rents would be when the building was completed. I leaned over and kissed her on the lips.

"What's that about?"

"I ache for what you're going through."

When we returned to the neighborhood, I invited her to my apartment, and since apartments were her main interest, she said she would like to see it. We entered and she walked directly to the nostalgia pieces.

"Wild," she said. "You invite women up to see your radio?"

"You're the first."

"Steve, I don't know how to tell you this. You're not just another guy from the neighborhood."

She went into the bedroom which I had decorated with white modern pieces.

"This is more my taste."

She put her hand on the bed to test the mattress. I was ready for her to ask how much I paid for it.

"It's a good bed," she said. "Do you want to make love?"

"Just like that?"

"Is that a—no?"

"Nancy! Do you have any idea what I went through in this neighborhood? Years of teenage torment. Breasts as far as the eye could see—untouched! Passion in hallways—unculminated! The maneuvering just to be alone with somebody, and the 'Please don'ts' and the 'No, Stevies.' And you just say, 'Do you want to make love?' Do you want to make love! I went through all that *then,* for it to be so easy *now?* It isn't fair!"

I was playing it to the hilt, a broader performance perhaps than even Arturo De Cordova in *Frenchman's Creek*. I was joking about it, but on some level I meant it.

"Jeannie Drago! Barbara Semmelman! All the rest! I prayed for actual, and I wasn't even close! And you say, 'Do you want to make love?' I mean, the answer is, yes, of course. But it isn't fair."

Chapter 18

I WAS NERVOUS THE first times with Nancy, concerned that her generation was going to have sexual secrets I could not decode. She was shy in sex, though, despite her original bravado, and not more experienced than I merely because she was younger.

We saw each other regularly on weekend evenings, usually going to the movies or to plays with tickets purchased at the cut-rate ticket stand on Times Square, and we became a foursome for dinners downtown with Jack and Terry. One night I entertained them all with dinner at my apartment, which I found in part pleasant and in part depressing, because it was a formalization of my bachelorhood.

Nancy had a degree in business administration from Manhattan College and wanted to make a career in banking. She was planning to take a master's degree at night to improve her prospects. First, she intended to change jobs when she found an apartment downtown.

Her prospective roommate was Patti Dempsey, also a cute brunette, a teller at the bank, about twenty-two soaking wet. They found a newsstand on West 12th Street in Manhattan where they could get the Sunday *New York Times* and the *Village Voice* early, and they met at 7 A.M. on Fordham Road every day like conspirators, checking the day's apartment listings in the daily newspaper, dividing up the city, going downtown to look at apartments and hurrying to be back at work by nine. Their momentum was certainly going to carry them right out of the Bronx.

In an interim act of independence Nancy arranged to spend a night at my place, which she had not done as yet. She told her parents she would be at a friend's house. "Dangerous sleeping around," she said, when she arrived with her overnight bag. "If my father ever found out, he'd kill me. He'd also kill *you*," she added, cheerfully.

In the morning I came out of the shower after one of my best "Be My Love"s in years. Nancy did not bother to look up from her reading.

"Mario Lanza," I said.

"Who?"

I feigned grief.

"Something ought to be done about the way they teach history these days."

On an evening in November, Sam was stricken with a heart attack and taken to Montefiore Hospital. Hinda phoned me at home and I went to see him. He was asleep, ashen, under oxygen. I stood there watching him and he awoke for a moment, saw me, nodded, then fell asleep again. I thought that at least I had seen him when he was still alive.

The connection it made for me was immediate. I went home and phoned my father.

"Dad?"

"How are you, Steve?"

"Good. I really called about you."

"I feel fine."

He told me he was the pitcher for a senior citizens' softball team, the league was for sixty-fives and over. In their most recent game he pitched an 18–15 victory, going all the way.

"I gave up only eleven hits, but there were twenty-two errors."

We said that we would get together soon, either I would come down to Florida or he would make a stopover in New York, since he and Rose were planning a trip to Israel.

"I still have the note you sent me," I said to him at the end of the call.

Sam made a recovery. Within a few days he was no longer receiving oxygen and the color returned to his face.

"I'm just not ready to meet the Big Bookie in the Sky," he joked when I went to visit him.

He was released from the hospital and in the weeks that followed I visited Sam at the apartment every day for an hour or so after work. I bought several sports board games and we would play during the dark winter afternoons. He was recuperating slowly and he looked forward to these games. Sports, which had been his passion, helped to sustain him now.

Nancy and I were D trains passing in the night. She found a job with Chemical Bank downtown and she and Patti located an apartment in the East Nineties. I volunteered to help them move and attached a U-haul trailer to my car. When we were finished loading their belongings, I bought a bottle of champagne and with paper cups we toasted The Great Escape.

"Here's to all the SOBs from one end of the Concourse to the other who ever did me dirty. Goodbye, forever," Nancy toasted.

"Here's to Frankie McCarthy in particular," Patti added, "who stood me up on a Christmas Eve to go out with Maureen Sheehy, who stuffed her bra with toilet paper."

"Here's to my Aunt Betty, who considers *Mary Poppins* a skin flick," Nancy said, "and what I am doing beyond redemption, even by papal decree. And while we're at it," Nancy continued, "here's to the Pope, a really cute guy, who's always welcome at our place."

I drove them to their apartment and helped them unload. They were so thrilled, I felt as though I were in on the releasing of two caged doves over the city. Nancy thanked me and kissed me at the door, apologizing for not being able to invite me to stay for the night, and for not wanting to go back to my apartment. "It's silly to go back there," she said. "I just came from there."

A few weeks later, Nancy and Patti had a housewarming party, and I went downtown with the Walshes. I had

not seen Nancy since she had moved—she told me she
had been busy with setting up the apartment and becoming adjusted to her new job. We walked into the party
and it occurred to me there could have been a product
called Instant Young People—a few drops of vodka and
they materialized to fill a room or an apartment. The
place was crowded with good-looking young people, male
and female, and I could not imagine how, in this short
period of time, Nancy and Patti had managed to meet so
many. Nancy greeted us and made introductions, to the
guys who lived upstairs, the girls who lived downstairs,
the guys and the girls from the bank, the friends of the
guys and girls from the bank, the friends of the friends.
Most of the time at the party, Jack, Terry and I, the out-
siders, talked to each other. I had a few minutes in the
kitchen with Nancy while she prepared hors d'oeuvres.
She was the center of attention of at least five males.
Probably concerned that I had been neglected, she introduced me to a fair, tall man in a suit and tie, in his early
thirties, one of the older men there.

"Steve, this is Ed. Ed—Steve. Ed's in advertising.
Steve used to be in advertising." And having made this
match she left us and went to welcome people who were
arriving.

"Where do you work, Ed?" I asked.

"Doyle Dane," he said imperiously.

"It's a good agency."

"That's true," he said, barely making eye contact with
me as he scanned the room for women.

"What do you do there?"

"Media."

"I see."

"She said *you* used to work in the field."

"Right."

"Where?"

"Robbins and Tolchin."

"Doing what?"

"Mostly copy."

"What are you doing now?" he asked, while looking over my shoulder at two young women who had just walked into the room.

"It's a lot to explain—"

I don't think he even heard me.

"Robbins and Tolchin, huh—" he said, tuning back in. "How are they doing since Robbins left?"

"I don't know. I've been away from it."

"Were you around when Robbins was there?" he asked offhandedly.

"We left at the same time," I said.

The men in the room were standing on line for Nancy's attention as though they were holding bakery tickets. I could see that I had just become someone from *her* past, a person from *her* old neighborhood. After a while the Walshes and I pushed our way through the crowd to say goodbye to Nancy and Patti and wish them luck. They were near the door with two young men who looked exactly like each other. I was finding that many of the young men at this party looked exactly like each other, but these particularly so—and then Patti told us they were twins. "Twin stockbrokers," she said. "Isn't that cute?"

"Does anybody here remember The Twin Cantors?" I asked. "I guess not."

New Year's Eve. Before this, the worst New Year's Eve for me was the time I had a date with Barbara Raskin, who told Arthur Pollack that she did not really like me and only made the date to get even with Richie Kastner, who was taking too long in asking her out, and we went downtown to the Van Cortlandt Hotel where the guys had rented a room for a bring-your-own-bottle party, with a portable phonograph playing, and when I took Barbara Raskin home, she shook hands with me at the door. That New Year's Eve was a tie with this one, as I lay in bed with the flu, alone in the Bronx, watching television and falling asleep before the ball dropped to start the 1980s, a date that gave me chills the flu could not even touch.

Ray Tolchin called to ask if we could meet for lunch. He had found out from Beverly that I was living in the Bronx, and I received a late night call from him, Tolchin sounding as if he had been drinking. I asked him to meet me at the candy store and he arrived by taxi this time.

"When you're a regular, you'll come by subway," I said. "How are you, Ray?"

"Are we eating here?" he said disdainfully.

"We can go to our local Lutece. Shannon's Bar."

"Fine. Just so long as I don't have to live through you serving me lunch."

I introduced Tolchin to Chris and then we walked over to Shannon's. The customers included a few construction workers and a house drunk. The luncheon menu consisted of frozen sandwiches, thawed in a toaster oven, and Cheez Doodles, which is why I usually ate in the store. One did not come to Shannon's for the cuisine. I ordered a grilled cheese and a Tab, Tolchin asked for a scotch on the rocks.

"I'll also spring for the grilled cheese," Tolchin said to O'Brien. "I'm sure it's a specialty of the house."

"Friend of yours?" O'Brien asked me.

"Ignore him. He's just ticked off because his credit card isn't good here."

Tolchin expressed his regrets about Beverly and me, then he told me about his latest program to ward off middle age—moonlight jogging with his new young girlfriend. When I told him that I had been jogging, he was interested in discussing distances and times. I did not think this was why he asked to see me. Eventually he looked around on all sides, leaned forward, and said, "Steve, I'd like to ask a favor of you." He removed an envelope from his jacket pocket.

"This is very confidential," he whispered.

"Whom do you think I would tell?" I whispered back.

He handed me the envelope, checking the room.

"Ray—nobody here is in your field!"

The envelope contained a proof sheet of an ad for the herbal tea company which had once been under my supervision. The ad showed a doctor examining a man, the copy consisting of nutritional information about tea.

"I need to know what you think."

"I feel like a Tibetan lama. You come uptown to seek truth?"

"Please, Steve. We've been arguing in the shop about it."

I looked at the ad.

"I don't know what the argument is. It's bad. It looks like a medical trade ad."

"That's what I thought. Shit!"

He ordered a second scotch.

"We're in trouble with the account, Steve. If you have any suggestions, I'd really appreciate it."

"Do you ever drink this tea?" I asked.

"No."

"It's good tea."

I examined the ad for a minute or two, then my mind drifted. I had looked at so many ads over the years, twenty years of trying to find the right clever phrase to win the day, twenty years of being zippy. I thought about the time when I had come out of the Bronx to learn that the Ivy Leaguers owned the court, how much I wanted to be like them, to pass in their world.

"What do you think, Steve?"

I focused my attention on the ad, and after a few minutes, I took a pen from Tolchin and wrote on a paper napkin:

"Once You Drink It, Regular Teas Taste Awful."

"I'd stress the taste," I said to Tolchin. "And I'd keep the nutritional stuff, but knock it way down in size. You could have a nice-looking person, arms folded, leaning on a whole display of the teas, looking right at you. I like the way 'awful' sounds. You don't see it in ads, so it could jump right out at you. 'Once you drink it, regular teas taste awful.'"

"It could work."

"I think so."

"It could work, you bastard! You rotten bastard! You solved it!" He was furious with me. "We're going crazy in the office and you just sit there and solve it!" In his anger, he grabbed my sleeve. "You bastard!"

O'Brien came rushing over from behind the bar.

"Take it easy," I said. "You're on my turf."

"You okay, Steve?" O'Brien asked.

"I'm fine. Right, Ray?"

"Yeah, he's fine," Tolchin said.

O'Brien went back to the bar, watching us.

"Steve, this is a waste! You have no right to be here."

"I do have a right."

"Look, we didn't see things the same way. Okay. We'll do it your way. You come back, we'll straighten everything out."

"I'm through with it, Ray. I don't get anything out of this anymore."

"You can be the president of an advertising agency! All you have to do is turn in your apron!"

"I'm sorry."

"You can't stay here! Who are you here?"

"Ray, if you run out of steam on what you've been doing all your working life, you're in trouble. I'm lucky they took me in."

"Come back, Steve. All is forgiven."

"That's my last ad. I'm finished with the zippy."

"How much can you make here for Chrissake? How much can you *ever* make that can top what you'll make with us?"

"I want to do something satisfying, Ray. If I make enough to earn a living, that's good enough."

"Steve, come on. Come back."

"No. It all goes too fast. It was the marbles season—and now I'm a middle-aged man."

Traffic in the store had slackened during the winter months, "We're forty-two egg creams behind August," Chris announced in a pained voice, going over his books. I tried to explain there had to be seasonal aspects to the business, not so many people were on the streets in the cold. He became obsessed with the weather and brought in a radio with a weather band station. "Egg creams will come back in the spring," I said. "They always do." Beyond that, I had nothing to offer. I had exhausted my ideas for improving the store. And I was beginning to experience cabin fever. It *was* slow in the store. The work was not enough for me. Tolchin's appearance had a lingering effect, "Who are you here?" he had said. I also recalled my mother's remarks from another time, "You can't be a soda jerk forever." And she was right.

"We have a real problem here," I told the dog. "This requires the help of an eminent caninist, such as yourself." Ramon did not reply, favoring a Freudian approach. "I feel that coming back here was good for me. Even having this job was good for me. So I don't think I made a mistake by coining back. What worries me is I might make a mistake by staying."

Neither of us had any suggestions. I decided it was time to walk my analyst.

I received a phone call at home from Sam's daughter, Claire. Sam had suffered another heart attack. This time he had died. Sam the Man.

The funeral service was held at Riverside Chapel on the Grand Concourse, attended by about forty people, relatives, friends. I went to Hinda when I entered the chapel, kissed her, and her eyes filled with tears.

"Stevie. He was so grateful for the time you spent with him."

"I liked being with him."

The rabbi was in his seventies and had known Sam for fifty years. After the traditional litanies, and after he spoke of the ways in which Sam would be remembered by the family, the rabbi said:

"Sam and I had a talk before he died. He told me that when his time came, I should stand before you and I should quote from a philosopher of whom he was especially fond—Leroy Satchel Paige."

He made us smile at his funeral. Who but Sam would have invoked Satchel Paige?

"Mr. Paige said, 'Keep the juices flowing by jangling around gently as you move. Go very lightly on the vices—the social ramble ain't restful. Avoid running at all times. And don't look back. Something might be gaining on you.'

"Sam Goodstein was a kind, gentle man," the rabbi continued. "He could have been many things, but he did in his life what he enjoyed. He did not look back at what might have been, or what he should have done. He was his own person. God rest his soul."

At Woodlawn Cemetery I stood behind the family as Sam's coffin was lowered into the earth. Then, as part of the day's ritual, I visited Hinda at the apartment afterward. When I was ready to leave, Hinda took me by the hand and led me to the door.

"We all wanted him to go to Florida, but he didn't want to."

"The Miami Dolphins. 'How can I root for a team that's the name of a fish?' "

"Also Claire was here, the grandchildren—and you were here, Stevie."

She opened the drawer of a bureau in the foyer.

"I know he'd want you to have something—"

"I couldn't have wanted anything better," I said, as she gave me the photograph taken in front of the candy store of Sam and myself at seventeen.

My link with the neighborhood as I had once known it was broken with Sam's passing. The new people I had met were leaving, Chris Anton, discontented, was making inquiries about luncheonettes in Queens, Jack and Terry were looking at garden apartments in Westchester, Nancy Reilly had already moved downtown. And I needed to "do better than a candy store," as my father had said. I needed to move on, to leave the neighborhood—just as I had done twenty years before. Only this time I was not ashamed of who I was, and where I came from.

Chapter 19

NEW NEIGHBORHOODS DO not have candy stores and the local coffee shop in the area where I had moved served liquor. My apartment was in the East Seventies of Manhattan, a renovated walk-up, a "junior three," the bedroom no more than a sleeping alcove. The area's most important architectural landmark was the newly enlarged frozen-food section of the nearby Gristede's supermarket. The console radio and the other nostalgia pieces I had brought with me from the Bronx took on an added radiance in the banal plasterboard box in which I now lived.

I found a jogging route along the East River, and I took long walks—Second and Third Avenues in the Seventies and Eighties appealed to me because the stores were eclectic and had some semblance of a neighborhood feeling. I stopped at an antiques store on Second Avenue to look at a windup phonograph in the window, but it predated the period for which I had been collecting pieces. Then I noticed several 78 rpm records in a stack and among them was "One Meat Ball" by Tony Pastor and His Orchestra. "One Meat Ball"! The great tragicomedy of the little man who went into a restaurant and could get no bread with one meat ball. I sang it in the shower before I ever heard of Mario Lanza.

"How much is this?"

The owner, a lanky blond man in his twenties, dragged himself out of his chaise to look at the recording.

"Fifteen dollars."

"You're kidding."

"That's what I can get for it."

" 'One Meat Ball.' Amazing. Did you ever hear this?"

"No."

"You never heard it? You don't even know what it is—and you're selling it for fifteen dollars?"

"I'm pretty busy now." No one else was in the store. "That's the price."

I bought it after first testing the record on the phonograph. Lyrical. I went home, delighted to have it, somewhat annoyed that I purchased it from a young man with no feeling for what he was selling, *and* he got his price. But you get no bread with one meat ball.

The idea did not come to me like a comic strip light bulb suddenly flashing above my head. I was living in Manhattan for several weeks without a clear plan as to what I would do for a living. I would have been content spending my time buying nostalgia pieces. This was not a way of paying the rent, though. Or was it? I wondered. Finding these old things had been so satisfying, I thought about the possibility of formalizing my interest—of making a business out of it. So I began going to junk shops, thrift shops and antiques stores in Manhattan and in Brooklyn, researching the kinds of things people were selling and how they were displayed. I learned from a dealer that a newspaper published in Connecticut called *The Newtown Bee* carried announcements of auctions and antiques shows which dealers from the Northeast attended. I went to a few of these events, checking the prices and the kinds of items that became available. Merchandise was less expensive outside of New York City and it seemed to me that if I could buy prudently, possibly I could resell the items in a store of my own in Manhattan. When I started to actually buy—to bid at auction and find pieces at shows and yard sales and country antiques shops—I became caught up in that particular kind of excitement that takes place with antiquing—in locating something neglected that has importance for you.

At a flea market in New Jersey, among his items, a man was selling souvenirs of the 1939 World's Fair and had a Heinz pickle pin. I had owned one of those very pins once, I had worn it on a cap.

"The price for this?"

"Ten dollars."

"I'll give you five."

"Seven."

I bought it for seven, wondering if I would be able to resell it for ten, and thinking—I found this. I haven't seen it in years and I'm holding it in my hand.

"You've got a steal," the dealer said. "You don't know the value of this."

"Yes, I do."

I traveled often now—to upstate New York, to New Jersey, to Pennsylvania, Connecticut, farther north into New England to country auctions and fairs, to yard sales and garage sales, to any place that had old items for sale. I wanted pieces from my own background, the things I remembered from the time when I was growing up. I was rescuing merchandise from cardboard cartons at rummage sales. I was on the grounds of country antiques shows in the dawn hours when dealers were arriving and had not yet unloaded their vans. I was negotiating with old ladies who had bridge tables set up in front of churches. Have dog, will travel. My apartment began to resemble the inside of a Santini Brothers' moving van, circa 1943.

I was able to make the purchases from the few thousand dollars I could count on after the agreements with Tolchin and Beverly—and when I reached the point where even the dog had to squeeze into the living room, I rented a long, narrow store on 75th Street between First and Second Avenues. I called the store "The Old Neighborhood."

When people walked into the place it would be as if they were stepping back in time. It was a gallery of treasures they might have thought they were never again to see. On the shelves were old radios, souvenirs of Edgar Bergen and Charlie McCarthy, maracas from Havana, bookends made of bronzed baby shoes, Orphan Annie and Captain Midnight decoders, glass picture frames with photos of stars like Brenda Marshall, rhinestone pins and Elgin watches, picture postcards from places long gone out of fashion, "Greetings from Coney Island," "Hello from Saratoga," 78 rpm records, The Andrews Sisters singing "Tico-Tico."

Furniture was arranged in room settings—overstuffed sofas and armchairs slipcovered with designs of palm leaves and oversized roses. And I had art deco lamps and clocks and serving dishes adorned with nymphs and pink flamingos. And there were toys that lasted forever, streamlined locomotives made of metal and airplanes with propellers that you could spin. And all around the store were advertising signs of the period, Burma-Shave, Bon Ami ("Hasn't scratched yet"), and posters from World War II including "The Four Freedoms" by Norman Rockwell.

On the wall behind the desk where I sat was a picture of George "Snuffy" Stirnweiss of the New York Yankees, and a framed snapshot taken in front of a candy store of a neighborhood bookie and a boy of seventeen. These items were not for sale.

I invited Sarah and Amy to come into New York so they could see the store and join me for a celebration brunch. We arranged this for the Sunday before the store opened officially, and they arrived at the apartment looking lovely, each in her own fashion, Amy without makeup, wearing a down vest, Sarah in a trenchcoat.

"I can't believe how beautiful you are," I said, kissing and hugging each of them, perhaps holding onto them a moment longer than they were comfortable with, but I missed them.

"You remember Ramon? My roommate and psycho-analyst."

"You're in therapy with your dog?" Sarah said, picking up on the remark. "Is that a new idea?"

"We're working on it."

"Glad to see you, señor Doctor," Amy said, shaking his paw.

The girls wandered through the apartment. The living room still had to function, in part, as a backup area for the store. I had six ice cream-parlor chairs standing there. I currently had more chairs in the living room than the number of people I knew.

"Are you expecting company, Daddy?" Sarah said.

"These are for the store."

"It's hard to get used to—your father's bachelor pad," Amy said, a forlorn expression on her face.

"It's hard for me, too, darling."

We went to a nearby pub for Sunday brunch, Sarah ordering a bloody Mary, if I needed any further evidence that she was a grownup. We talked for a while, Sarah was considering changing her major from drama to political science, Amy was leaning toward geology, and then the conversation became forced, there was a growing tension in all of us as the meal neared the end. We were getting to the time when they would have to see the store. They were obviously concerned that this new idea of mine was also going to embarrass them. As for me, these were my children, I did not need their permission for my decisions, but I loved them and I did not want them to think I was a fool.

I had placed brown paper on the windows of the store

so people could not see inside while I was working. The paper was still hanging and the girls had to wait for me to open the door before they could see the store. Out of tension, none of us had spoken for the last three blocks. I unlocked the door, turned on the lights, they stepped inside, and Sarah, my cool reserved child, began to cry.

"Daddy—it's wonderful. It's just wonderful," and she placed her head against me. "I was so worried."

"It's fabulous," Amy said. "We didn't know what to expect."

"Well, you're the first to see it."

"Congratulations, Daddy," Sarah said.

"Yes, Daddy, congratulations. Where did you get all this stuff?"

"That's a lot of the fun—finding it."

And I took them through the store, showing them the kinds of things I had grown up with—including a set of blue glass dinnerware, "There was something called 'Dish Night' at the movies . . ." and the posters, "These were very powerful images in their time. . . ." They were attentive. They were happy for me. I was not a fool.

On Opening Day, my first buyer was a middle-aged woman who bought a 1939 World's Fair ashtray. The sequence was exactly as I wanted it to be—I picked out the ashtray because it had made an emotional connection for me and she bought it because the connection was made for her.

"Going to the Fair was one of the greatest days of my life," she said, remembering. "My father took me and I felt like a princess."

I received a telegram at the store from Beverly:

"I wish you much luck and with all my heart I hope you will be happy. Keep this telegram. Maybe it will be worth something one day, Beverly."

The store gave me the action I needed, I could buy and sell and trade, and it was never just merchandise to me. I loved these old things. I loved their character and their texture. I continued going out into the countryside to find items, and people began to search me out to sell or trade. My customers were varied—passersby from the area, interior decorators, art directors, young women buying pins and jewelry for fashion, middle-aged and older people looking for pieces out of their pasts—and collectors. I was fascinated by the kinds of collections people owned—people collected only campaign buttons, only Roosevelt buttons, only radios, dog people wanted only dog items, "Got any Rin Tin Tin?" People collected for their professions, "Got anything about dentists?"

My father and Rose came north en route to Israel and stayed in a hotel in Manhattan for a few days. They seemed to like the store. "Now you've got something," my father said when he saw it. When Rose was off shopping in the afternoons, my father sat in the store with me. The atmosphere made him nostalgic about *his* old days.

"When we first moved to the Bronx, it was like a miracle to us—coming from the Lower East Side. The Concourse, the trees. We thought you'd have a good place to grow up."

"I did."

A young woman in her twenties came in and was intrigued with the set of blue glass dinnerware. My policy was to avoid hard sell. I felt an item had to make an emotional connection for the customer, except with people too young to remember, and in those cases I offered whatever information I could. I told her about "Dish Night" and that I was amused to see this type of dinnerware was now being called "Depression glass." A book had been published on the subject which I had in the store and showed her. She decided to buy the dishes as a gift for her parents.

"You're a good salesman. And you're honest," my father said when she had left. "You know, I never thought *I* was a good salesman—because I never made store manager. Now I think maybe I *was* pretty good. I mean, I always had a job."

"And people respected you."

"They did. I just never sold anybody anything that wasn't right, that's all."

As we sat there in the store I never felt so close to him. I remembered how he always was honest in his work, and I realized, in terms of my own integrity, that what I really had wanted to be was a person like my father.

My divorce was soon to be final, the divorce agreement was going "amicably," my lawyer had said. I had a conversation over the phone with Beverly—details about things in the house, and I thanked her for the telegram she had sent.

"Are you happy there?" she asked.

"Yes. I am."

"I'm glad, Steve."

"When we talk next, we'll be divorced," I said.

"We're still talking. That's better than some."

"It's strange. It's as if we just—ran out of time. Like those old radio shows. You were into it and all of a sudden they were signing off. 'We're a little late, folks, so goodnight.' I paused, finding it difficult to speak. 'Say goodnight, Bevvy.' "

"Goodnight, Bevvy," she said quietly, on the beat.

Beverly and I have little to do with each other now— "amicable," but "divorced." Sarah and Amy have stayed in my life, which, I suppose, is the best a parent can hope for with a divorce and with children who are becoming adults. They like to come to the store when they are in New York, and they even have had dates call for them there, which I accept as a sign of my respectability.

Jack Walsh and I have spoken, the Saturday softball games will be starting again, he will be traveling down from Westchester and I can have right field back if I want it, and I do.

The main industry in my present neighborhood appears to be singles bars. I am having difficulty with the marketing of myself in this field. I tried three of these places and have yet to finish a drink in any of them. And I still think of Beverly. But there are one or two women who have been into the shop whom I am about to approach socially. I think I have as good a story to tell as the competition.

The business keeps improving, and I look forward to my days. I am learning to live on less income than I

earned at the agency, but I have no regrets about leaving advertising. I like to think that with the store I am
a kind of custodian of people's memories—I find things
that might be lost or forgotten and I pass them on.

Recently I located a set of the original *Classic Comics,*
an early copy of *Lad, a Dog,* by Albert Payson Terhune
and a team photo of the 1947 Brooklyn Dodgers. Some of
these things are getting more valuable as they get older,
and, perhaps, so am I.

Excerpts from other novels

by Avery Corman

from Barricade Books

A great read, breezy but detailed and candid, with great dialogue."
Dave Eggers

kramer

vs.

kramer

Avery Corman

The groundbreaking novel
adapted into the
Academy Award-winning Best Picture

**The best-selling novel
that transformed divorce and child custody.
Adapted into the Academy Award-winning Best Picture
starring Dustin Hoffman and Meryl Streep,
winner of five Academy Awards.**

"You don't do it this way, Joanna. Not like this."

"Why not?"

"You do something else first. We should talk to somebody, see somebody."

"I know about therapists. Most of them are middleclass people with a personal stake in marriage."

"What are you saying?"

"I said it. I've got to get out. I'm getting out."

"Joanna — "

"Feminists will applaud me."

"What feminists? I don't see any feminists."

"I'm going, Ted."

"To where, for crying out loud?"

"I don't know."

"You don't know?"

"It doesn't even matter."

"*What?*"

"That's right. Is it getting through to you?"

"Joanna, I hear this happening to other people. I don't believe it's happening to us. Not like this. You just don't make an announcement like this."

"What difference does it make how I tell you? I was going to leave a note. Maybe I should have."

"What are we, in grade school? You're breaking up with your old Valentine chum? We're married people!"

"I don't love you, Ted. I hate my life. I hate being here. I'm under so much pressure I think my head is going to explode."

"Joanna — "

"I don't want to be here another day, not another minute."

"I'll get the name of somebody. A marriage counselor, somebody. There's a more rational way of dealing with this."

"You're not hearing me, Ted. You never hear me. I'm going. I've gone already."

"Listen, I think sometimes I've been too involved with work. And my mind's been on that. I'm sorry for it."

"Ted, that's nothing. It doesn't mean anything. This has nothing to do with where you are — it's me. I can't live like this. I'm finished with it. I need a new place for myself."

"So what are we supposed to do? I mean, how do you do this? Am I supposed to move out? Is there another guy? Does he move in?"

"You don't understand anything, do you?"

"I mean, you have all this worked out. What do we do, goddammit?"

"I take my bags, which are packed, and two thousand dollars from our joint savings account, and I leave."

"You leave? What about Billy? Do we wake him? Are his bags packed?"

For the first time in this, she faltered.

"No . . . I . . . I'm not taking Billy. He'll be better off without me."

"Christ, Joanna! Joanna!"

She could not say another word. She walked into the bedroom, picked up her suitcase and her racquet bag, walked to the front door, opened it and left. Ted stood there, watching. He was bewildered. He seriously thought she would be back in an hour.

oh, God!

Avery Corman

The classic comic novel
adapted into the hit movie comedy
by the author of Kramer vs. Kramer

"I'll tell you why I'm doing this," He said. "They've been going around saying I'm dead or worse."

"What's worse?"

"That I never was, or what I was was gas or *shmutz*."

"*Shmutz*?"

"You know, particles. With the big bang theories and the little bang theories. When you're God, it's insulting."

He was confiding in me!

"Let's stop right here. I really think you should be talking to somebody higher up. The Pope maybe."

"No, I looked into this. And you're my fella."

I'm His fella! What if I don't ask the right questions? What if I misquote Him? A misquote here has cosmic significance.

"Excuse me. What do I call you?"

"Call me God."

"God, I think I should have a tape recorder."

"Forget it. It wouldn't work."

"Why?"

"My voice—it wouldn't come out on the tape."

"I don't understand."

"I can't go into it. It's very complex. It's like... what would you understand? Ghosts. You know how they used to say a ghost was not supposed to cast a shadow? Well, it's like that. You can't record God's voice."

"I really don't understand."

"*Oy-oy-oy*," He said. "Because it's not my real voice. I'm just making this up for you, so you can hear it. I mean, I'm God over everybody, but I'm not speaking Chinese, am I?"

"Actually, you sound a little Jewish."

"What then? You're a little Jewish, aren't you?"

"Yes."

"So like I'm telling you, I'm doing this for you. By the way, I was at your Bar Mitzvah. It didn't knock me out."

"You were there?"

"I'm there for everything—prayers, weddings, Bar Mitzvahs, funerals, baptisms—you name it. 'The Pledge of Allegiance' to the flag with that *under God* thing in it—I'm there. A fella stubs his toe and says 'goddammit'—I'm there. Kate Smith sings 'God Bless America'—I'm there."

"That's an incredible concept. That's something Man has wanted to know for centuries. Are prayers heard? Does God listen?"

"Who says I listen? I only said I'm there. After a while, who can listen?"

"Then God *doesn't* care."

"I care. I care plenty. But what can I do?"

"But you're God."

"Only for The Big Picture."

"What?"

"I don't get into details."

"Why?"

"It's better that I shouldn't meddle. What am I going to do—get into favorites? So I come up with the concepts, the big ideas—the details can take care of themselves."

"Then the way things happen on earth..."

"They happen. Don't look at me."

"And there's no plan, no scheme that controls our destinies?"

"A lot of it is luck. Luck and who you know."

a

perfect

divorce

Avery Corman

The wise and moving novel
by the author of Kramer vs. Kramer

Kim Greenley was crying. The word spread through the classrooms, the corridors, and by evening nearly all of the 125 seniors at The Bantrey School and a substantial number of parents knew that Kim Greenley, a B-plus student, whose rendition on Music Night of *When I Marry Mister Snow* had received a standing ovation, whose father was an orthopedist and whose mother was an administrator at Lenox Hill Hospital—how bona fide can parents be—Kim Greenley, of the sweet, round face and blue eyes, a little chubby perhaps, but why should that matter, Kim Greenley, with a boyfriend at Cornell, which placed her off limits to the boys and nonthreatening to the girls, bright, likable with serious credentials, left the office of the college advisor for the crucial beginning-of-senior-year college assessment meeting, crying. Her parents solemnly followed her, the father biting his bottom lip, the mother grim and looking close to tears herself. Outside the advisor's door they paused for a few words between themselves along the lines of how could this possibly happen, as Kim moved on, shaken.

The next group waited on an oak bench, Karen and Rob Burrows and Tommy, their seventeen-year-old son. Tommy had known Kim since kindergarten and rushed over to her before she descended the stairs out of the building, wanting to offer solace, something; her parents had momentarily abandoned her. She looked at him through wet eyes, her world collapsing.

"Tommy, he said I'll never get into Brown."

The Burrows family was on deck to see the college advisor with this bleak foreshadowing, like the Lenny Bruce routine of the comic who bombs at the London Palladium, the comic just about to go on and the female singer on stage ahead of him asks the audience for a moment of silence for the boys who went to Dunkirk and never came back. Not a good sign for the Burrows group, this Kim Greenley business. The advisor's secretary, a middle-aged woman of no discernible charm, appeared poker-faced as in I've-seen-them-cry-before, and said, "Mr. Kammler will see you now."

"So, Tommy, Mr. and Mrs. Burrows," the voice, warm, friendly, a paradox considering the verdicts rendered here.

"I see your grades are pretty consistently C pluses and B minuses."

"Could be I'll do better this year." The remark for appearance's sake. He had no expectation of doing better in his senior year. He did what he did year after year, an average student at Bantrey with no peaks and no valleys, but no peaks.

Afterward, Karen and Rob paused a moment before parting and looked into each other's eyes with sadness—this is our boy, his first words, his first steps, his first everything belonged to another time, as did innocence. Not only of their love, but of Tommy himself and who he was—and now this professional was saying, by the standards used to measure these young people, he was not on the level of his peers. So there was disappointment, but they loved his kindness, they loved his wit, they loved his physical grace, they loved him. Whatever the direction of their lives, he was of them, born when they were special together, and in the rush of these shared feelings, Rob leaned over and kissed Karen on the forehead. It was the first time they had touched in any meaningful way in four years.

50

Avery Corman

The compelling novel about midlife
and time passing
by the author of Kramer vs. Kramer

After the eye examination Doug Gardner sat across from Dr. Jeffrey Weiss in an office so dark with its heavy leather furniture, murky brown wallpaper and dim lighting, the only good light a desk lamp on the doctor's desk, he thought it might have been a psychological ploy. Everyone leaves here thinking he's going blind and is, therefore, in desperate need of Dr. Weiss's ophthalmology. Weiss was trim, about six feet tall, with a full head of blond hair. He was probably one of those people who regularly passed Doug on the jogging track in Central Park while Doug slogged along. Everyone passed him. Doug loathed jogging and did it because of the articles, all that evidence about cardiovascular benefits that will keep you alive longer. Nobody gave you an actual number, though. Will one thousand miles of tedious jogging give you an extra six days, six weeks? And when do you get your jogger's bonus, he wondered. Now, when you're still able to eat a pastrami sandwich, or at the end when you're already on a life-support system?

"When was your last eye examination?" Dr. Weiss asked in a sharp tone.

Doug judged this dour man to be his late 30s. The problem, suddenly, was not the headaches from the eye strain or that he was holding his reading matter so far away he was running out of arm length—it was that he was getting older than the doctors.

"About five years ago," Doug said.

"Five years?" Dr. Weiss responded with disapproval. "You shouldn't wait five years at your age, Mr. Gardner."

"For anything?"

Dr. Weiss did not smile at Doug's remark. What does this mean? Does he have dire information on his pad?

"You have a typical diminution of focusing abilities for your age group," the doctor said charmlessly. "Middle-age eyes, I call it. You need reading glasses."

"Just for reading?"

"Yes. But I'd like to make a suggestion. If you engage in any sports involving a ball, racquetball, tennis, buy yourself a shatterproof eye guard. You'd be surprised at how many men your age I see with serious eye injuries. Let's face it, your eye-hand coordination starts to go, too."

"This is turning out to be more than I want to know on the subject."

"I'm just being factual, Mr. Gardner."

"Yes, I get that,"

"I'll write you a prescription for the glasses. I suggest you make an appointment to come back in six months."

Did he have to add the part about eye-hand coordination? Doug had good eyes once, the Eddie Stanky of his day, with an ability to wait patiently and foul off pitches for walks. As he headed along crowded Forty-second Street in Manhattan, another of the people with poor posture, their faces drawn with New York tension, he conceded that getting bases on balls was no longer a marketable skill for him. He hadn't prided himself on not wearing glasses, the idea of glasses never occurred to him one way or another. Now that he had to wear them and would continue to have headaches if he did not, he felt as if he were starting to creak, a tin man needing oil.

the bust-out king

Avery Corman

The rollicking comic novel of a nefarious uncle,
Uncle Rocco, and his besieged nephew, Joseph—
Rocco exposing Joseph to the world of the scam,
the caper, the bust-out.

Our wedding reception was held at the Concourse Plaza Hotel, a small gathering since neither of our families was very large or very rich. There was some discussion in my house whether my Uncle Rocco, my father's younger brother, would show up for the wedding, since no one had seen Uncle Rocco in several years. Uncle Rocco did not appear, but several weeks later, Mary Anne and I did receive a wedding gift from him.

A strange, rugged man appeared at our door, wearing dark glasses and a black raincoat turned up at the collar, hardly your average United Parcel person.

"Joseph Farroni?" he said, almost as an accusation.

"Yes?" I answered warily.

"Dis is from ya Uncle Rocco."

And he pushed a large box into the apartment and left.

We opened the box. It contained twenty-four identical Waring blenders. Which was typical of Uncle Rocco.

I saw him only twice in my life that I clearly remember. When I was eight years old, my family rented a small bungalow in Rockaway Park, near the ocean. One day my sister and I saw a Lincoln Continental parked in front of the house and, leaning against the car, two muscular men. We went inside, and standing there with my parents was a short, stocky man, balding, dark complexioned, narrow, intense eyes, and a prominent nose like my father's and mine. He was smoking a big cigar and wearing a matching silk cabana outfit with Hawaiian scenes all over it. But on his feet he wore ordinary black socks and black leather street shoes, as though he had put on a beach outfit appropriate for his visit and had not been concerned with this last detail.

"This is your Uncle Rocco," my father said.

"What do you say, kids?" he said. "Salvatore?" My father shook his head emphatically, no. Rocco nodded and then walked over to a suitcase he had placed on the dining room table.

"Okay, then Salvatore. You take care, kids." He opened the suitcase slightly. "Here. Have a good time. Go on the rides."

And from the suitcase he handed each of us a $20 bill. I managed a quick glance and saw that the suitcase was stuffed with money. Then, in an elegant manner, he shook hands with my father, kissed my mother, kissed my sister, shook hands with me, and briskly walked out the door, carrying his suitcase, in his silk Hawaiian outfit with the black leather shoes.

Over the years, I would receive gifts from him at random times or at Christmas. Not the customary gifts an uncle might send a nephew, like a football or a basketball. I would receive a shipment of eighteen footballs, twelve basketballs, as though Uncle Rocco had suddenly cornered a market on them.

When I was nineteen and in college, I was walking along Broadway one day and a long, black chauffeured limousine pulled alongside of me.

"Hey, kid!" someone yelled from the back seat. It was Uncle Rocco. He whispered something to the driver, who stopped the car, got out, went to the trunk of the car, put some boxes in a shopping bag and handed it to me. Uncle Rocco just sat there.

The driver quickly got back in the car, and as they drove away, Uncle Rocco called out, "Merry Christmas!" It was the middle of April. In the shopping bag were sixteen electric shavers.

the
big
hype

Avery Corman

At times I felt like the bear in the penny arcade game who scurried back and forth and spun around when you hit the target. I was a bicoastal bear going back and forth between the Polo Lounge in Beverly Hills and the Russian Tea Room in New York.

I worked as a television scriptwriter and had written about forty scripts for television dramas. It was an unending struggle to find interesting projects to work on, so I was constantly in meetings with people, pitching ideas I wanted to write, listening to their proposals. I had won four Emmys and each of those movies for television went on to another life in videocassettes. Several producers referred to me as their "quality guy" and without embarrassment actually used that expression in conversation. I was "doing well" in my work, but like many scriptwriters, I was writing The Novel on the side. A two-month period when I was able to work on the book was coming to an end; I needed a television assignment for money again, so it was time to put on my bear outfit and scurry for work.

My immediate hope was Tod Martin, a producer in from the West Coast. These California producers were so tan and healthy-looking that as a New Yorker sitting opposite them, I thought that I looked like a character in a black and white movie who had been colorized imperfectly and turned out faintly green.

I had worked with Tod Martin before on a worthwhile project about the Wright Brothers. He had called, eager to offer me an assignment so important, he said, that he had to present it to me face to face. We met for lunch in the Russian Tea Room, the tanned one and the green one. Martin was a rangy man in his late thirties, six feet two, in a pink cashmere sweater and white slacks, shirt open at the neck.

"Paul, I'm offering you my best," he said. "A movie special for ABC. I have a go."

"Good, Tod."

"It's scary, but quality. You ready for this? Lyme Disease!"

He leaned back, self-satisfied, allowing me to savor the beauty of his suggestion.

"Tod, I appreciate the thought, but—"

"We're going first class on this one. That's why I called my quality guy. We do it as a medical mystery. You know, like it's transmitted to somebody from the family dog and somebody's sick, but they don't know how or why."

"Lyme disease. You're making me itch."

"*That's* what we're looking for, that kind of involvement. People sitting in front of their sets, scratching, looking at their dogs funny."

"Let me rise to the occasion," I said. "The closing shot is like that last image from *Viva Zapata* where the white horse lives on in the hills. The last thing you see is the family dog, a cocker spaniel, roaming the grounds of a house rendered vacant by the disease."

"That's goddamn poetic."

"No, I didn't mean it. It's a lousy illness to get and I don't want to do this kind of work."

"You pass?"

"I pass. The hives that await me if I did it—the dermatologist's bills alone wouldn't make it worth my while."

prized

possessions

Avery Corman

The powerful novel about
a college campus date rape
by the author of Kramer vs. Kramer

**The deeply involving novel about a rape,
as the lives of the victim,
the accused, and the families are shattered.**

She wanted to melt into the crowd, be anonymous. *He* was around, though. A senior, he wouldn't be in any of her classes, but she might see him. And he might be bragging. She couldn't bear that, Jimmy Andrews telling buddies how she was a notch on his belt. She located his number through information and called.

"Hello," he said.

"This is Liz."

"Well, hi."

"Maybe I should have you arrested—"

"What?"

"Listen carefully to what I have to say. Don't you dare tell anybody you know that you 'made it' with me. I don't want you bragging. If I hear anything, if I see any of your wonderful pals looking at me with knowing glances—"

"Liz, look, it didn't go so smoothly. Maybe we should try again. Get a better rhythm with each other."

"I can't believe how disgusting you are. Don't you ever look at me or speak to me again."

Her mother called. She told her she was fine. No, there was nothing wrong with her voice; it was probably the connection. Her father came on the line. Everything was fine. She would call later in the week. It was nice talking to them. She chose not to say; Oh, by the way, I was raped. It's true I had a couple of beers and necked with him, but I said no, I pleaded with him, I screamed, and he grabbed me by my throat and jammed my legs open, and he pushed himself into me again and again. And how have you been, Mom and Dad?

Her faculty advisor was Cynthia Moss, from the music department. "You were supposed to be a music major. A music major takes music."

"I'm rethinking things."

"I'm hard pressed to know what the point is in continuing to attend vocal classes without singing."

"Then I should drop the course."

"Is that what you want?"

"Definitely."

"I trust that you'll resume in the spring." She used her glasses to punctuate the remark.

"I can't say."

"Adjustments are often difficult for new students. We have a college psychologist. I'd like you to see her."

"Is she going to tell me, 'Sing out, Louise'?"

"What?"

What? What do you want to hear? That I'm damaged goods and the thought of standing up in front of people and presenting myself as cute and perky, and singing, *singing* of all things, as though I were a cheery little bird, is so ridiculous that I can't even think about it. Is that what I should say to you?

Intellectually, Elizabeth consigned the rape to the category of nightmares in order to distance herself from it. This did not stop it from violating her sleep in real nightmares. In her dreams a figure hovered over her and she couldn't breathe. She would violently throw herself out of sleep, sweating, gasping for breath. The bad images came in the day, too, flickering across her consciousness during her waking hours, triggered by random suggestions of sexuality: a boy in one of her classes who looked at her with interest, a girl on a lawn sitting with a boy, flirting with him. These occurrences would provoke the event to return like a hideous rodent that kept darting across her path.

the
boyfriend
from
hell

Avery Corman

The romantic psychological thriller
by the author of Kramer vs. Kramer

**The spirit of *Sex and the City* and *Girls*
blended wih the terror of *Rosemary's Baby*
in this spellbinding romantic pyschological thriller.**

Alex was not the most efficient doorman in New York, famous for forgetting to give people packages or for giving people the wrong packages.

"Something for you, Miss Delaney," and he handed over a white box tied with a green ribbon. There wasn't any indication who sent it, just an index card with Ronnie Delaney's name written on it.

"Do you know who this is from?"

"I didn't see anybody. It was left outside the door."

"Thank you, Alex."

He was pleased. He got the right package to the right person.

They went up to the apartment, Bob took a can of soda from the refrigerator. Nancy went into the bedroom, and Ronnie sat at the dining table and opened the box. She saw no card on top of the white tissue inside. Her scream brought Bob and Nancy running into the room. Inside the box was a dead black cat.

The police officers asked some preliminary questions, one of them took notes, and the officers went downstairs so that the doorman could be interrogated.

"This is obviously a prank," one of the officers said when they came back into the apartment.

"It's a death threat," Ronnie said flatly.

"I'm an attorney," Bob said, backing her. "Not a criminal attorney, but nonetheless an attorney and I think you gentlemen have to raise the level of concern here."

"I write an article about a satanic cult and I get a dead black cat in a box. I take this very seriously," Ronnie said.

The police officers left and an hour and a half later two plainclothes detectives came to the apartment, Detective Ralph Gomez and Detective Fred Santini. They were on another level of police work, which was largely dour.

After taking down the basic information Santini asked, "Is it possible, Ms. Delaney, it wasn't this cult guy who sent this?"

"Then one of his people," Ronnie said. "He's got about a thousand of them. For all I know they've got dead black cats stacked up like in a wine cellar."

"May I see the article?" Gomez said.

Ronnie produced a copy of *New York* magazine.

"May we have this?" Gomez asked.

"By all means."

"How long is this going to take?" Nancy said. "We've got a person here somebody tried to terrorize. I mean, are you going to get right on it?"

"We're on it right now, aren't we?" Gomez said.

"I guess we all want to know how this works, what the procedures are," Bob said.

"We'll take the box, determine cause of death of this cat, which conceivably could give us something," Santini said. "Check for prints. Did any of you handle the box?"

"Just me and the doorman."

"We'll get your prints, if you don't mind," Gomez said. "And your doorman, and see what else is on it. My guess, there won't be anything else. Somebody does this, they don't leave prints."

"How would you know?" Ronnie said. "Have you had any experiences like this?"

"Not precisely the same. But—things go on."

"Ms. Delaney, anyone you're on the outs with? Like an old boyfriend?" Santini asked.

"I did have a boyfriend, but I assure you this is not his style.